His Best Friend

PATRICIA KAY

D0039278

Silhouette®

SPECIAL EDITION®

Published by Silhouette Books

America's Publisher of Contemporary Romance

This book is dedicated, with thanks, to the
supportive staff at my local CURVES.
You've made a big difference in my life!

 SILHOUETTE BOOKS

ISBN 0-373-24660-9

HIS BEST FRIEND

Copyright © 2005 by Patricia A. Kay

This edition published by arrangement with Harlequin Books S.A.

® and TM are trademarks of Harlequin Books S.A., used under license.
Trademarks indicated with ® are registered in the United States Patent
and Trademark Office, the Canadian Trade Marks Office and in other
countries.

Visit Silhouette Books at www.eHarlequin.com

Printed in U.S.A.

John couldn't believe his eyes.

Philip's date was the blonde! The one John had met in Austin.

She'd recognized him, too. He could see the surprise in her eyes.

Philip proudly drew the blonde forward. "John, this is Claudia Hathaway, the new prof I was telling you about. Claudia, my cousin John Renzo."

She tilted her head, studying John. "Actually, I believe we've met."

"You've met?" Philip looked from one to the other.

John shrugged. "But I didn't know her name." He couldn't stop staring at her. God, she was even more gorgeous than he'd remembered. Tonight, in that black clingy outfit, she looked fantastic. Although she was lean, her body was sexy, with curves in the right places. And she was the wonderful Claudia that Philip had been talking about for weeks?

How was that possible?

Dear Reader,

Well, we hope your New Year's resolutions included reading some fabulous new books—because we can provide the reading material! We begin with *Stranded with the Groom* by Christine Rimmer, part of our new MONTANA MAVERICKS: GOLD RUSH GROOMS miniseries. When a staged wedding reenactment turns into the real thing, can the actual honeymoon be far behind? Tune in next month for the next installment in this exciting new continuity.

Victoria Pade concludes her NORTHBRIDGE NUPTIALS miniseries with *Having the Bachelor's Baby,* in which a woman trying to push aside memories of her one night of passion with the town's former bad boy finds herself left with one little reminder of that encounter—she's pregnant with his child. Judy Duarte begins her new miniseries, BAYSIDE BACHELORS, with *Hailey's Hero,* featuring a cautious woman who finds herself losing her heart to a rugged rebel who might break it…. THE HATHAWAYS OF MORGAN CREEK by Patricia Kay continues with *His Best Friend,* in which a woman is torn between two men—the one she really wants, and the one to whom he owes his life. Mary J. Forbes's sophomore Special Edition is *A Father, Again,* featuring a grown-up reunion between a single mother and her teenaged crush. And a disabled child, an exhausted mother and a down-but-not-out rodeo hero all come together in a big way, in Christine Wenger's debut novel, *The Cowboy Way.*

So enjoy, and come back next month for six compelling new novels, from Silhouette Special Edition.

Happy New Year!

Gail Chasan
Senior Editor
Silhouette Special Edition

Please address questions and book requests to:
Silhouette Reader Service
U.S.: 3010 Walden Ave., P.O. Box 1325, Buffalo, NY 14269
Canadian: P.O. Box 609, Fort Erie, Ont. L2A 5X3

PATRICIA KAY,

formerly writing as Trisha Alexander, is the *USA TODAY* bestselling author of more that thirty contemporary romances. She lives in Houston, Texas. To learn more about her, visit her Web site at www.patriciakay.com.

CAST OF CHARACTERS—
The Hathaways of Morgan Creek

Stella Morgan Hathaway (91 years old)—Matriarch of the Hathaway family. Morgan Creek is named after her great-grandfather Jeremiah Morgan. A strong, domineering woman, she is used to controlling her family and their lives.

Jonathan Morgan Hathaway (68 years old)—Her only son.

Kathleen Bryce Hathaway (64 years old)—Jonathan's wife.

Bryce Hathaway (41 years old)—Jonathan and Kathleen's only son, he heads the family business and recently married Amy Jordan.

Amy Hathaway (33 years old)—Bryce's wife, she has brought happiness back into his life.

Calista Hathaway (4 years old)—Amy's daughter from her first marriage, recently adopted by Bryce.

Chloe Hathaway Standish (37 years old)—The oldest Hathaway daughter.

Lorna Morgan Hathaway (33 years old)—The middle Hathaway daughter.

Claudia Elizabeth Hathaway (29 years old)—The youngest Hathaway daughter.

Greg Standish (39 years old)—Chloe's husband.

Cameron Kathleen Standish (15 years old)—Chloe and Greg's daughter.

Stella Ann Hathaway (9 years old)—Bryce's oldest daughter.

Susan Adele Hathaway (8 years old)—Bryce's youngest daughter.

Prologue

Claudia Hathaway decided to drive to Austin and spend the day with Sally Bennett, her best friend from college days at U.T. They would shop till they dropped, hitting all the trendiest places, have a fab lunch, then catch a chick flick.

"Oh, Claudia, I hate that you're moving to Houston," Sally wailed as she hugged Claudia hello. "We're never gonna see each other anymore."

Claudia rolled her eyes. "It's not the end of the world, Sally. Houston's only three hours away, less if I live near Highway 290." She squeezed her friend's shoulder. "It's not like I live next door now. I mean, it takes me almost an hour to get here."

"I know, but it just seems so *far.*"

"We'll just have to fix firm dates to see each other. One month I'll come up here and the next you'll visit me there." Claudia couldn't help it. She was so excited about her new job and the move to Houston, it was hard for her to sympathize with Sally. Besides, what she'd said was true. Houston wasn't that far away. "Now c'mon, cheer up. Let's hit those sales."

End-of-summer sales at Austin stores were always terrific, and that day was no exception. Claudia bought several pairs of nice slacks, a couple of summer sweaters and two jackets—one in a nubby black linen, the other a silk weave in a gorgeous shade the salesclerk called claret. Claudia justified her extravagance by telling herself she could wear all the new clothes on the job, and college professors needed to look good, didn't they?

She and Sally decided on lunch at a trendy new restaurant overlooking the water on Town Lake. The place had been recently written up in *Texas Monthly* magazine, and supposedly the crab cakes were to die for.

After they'd placed their order and Sally had flirted shamelessly with their handsome waiter, she turned her attention back to Claudia and what was now becoming her favorite point of contention.

"I just don't see why you didn't look for a job in Austin. We could have had so much fun together if you lived here." This was followed by a put-upon sigh.

Claudia smothered her own sigh. She loved Sally like a sister, but sometimes Sally strained her patience. However, Sally was her best friend and had supported her when she needed support, so she didn't allow her impatience to show in her voice. "I agree it *would* be fun to live near you. Unfortunately, you live too near Morgan Creek. If I lived in Austin, I'd never have any peace. It'd be just like it was when I was in college. I'd still be expected home for Sunday dinner. My mother would constantly grill me on who I was dating. And my grandmother would never stop bugging me about not working for the company." The company was Hathaway Baking, one of the largest and most successful baking companies in the Texas/Oklahoma area.

"I know." But Sally still sounded glum.

"And no matter how many times I told them, especially Gran, that I *hate* the business world and that my decision had *nothing* to do with our company and everything to do with the fact I'm just not cut out to work in business, she just will never accept it. So the best thing for me to do is what I'm doing—putting some distance between me and my well-meaning but extremely irritating family." She grinned to soften her words, because no matter how irritating some of her family members could be, she genuinely loved them and knew she would miss them.

"I would think by now you'd be used to your grandmother. I mean, she always wants her own way, you know that."

"Yes, but it still gets old listening to her. Not only old, but dangerous. 'Cause, eventually, if you're subjected to her gloves of steel long enough, you start weakening, and before you know it, you're doing exactly what she wants you to do. No, I've made the right decision. I love Gran, but she's too stubborn and she knows exactly how to layer on the guilt until a person has no willpower left." Out of the corner of her eye, Claudia saw their waiter approaching with their drinks. "Now c'mon, let's change the subject and talk about something fun."

For the rest of their meal, Claudia's approaching move wasn't discussed. Instead, they talked about mutual friends, Sally's dating life, which—according to her—was practically nonexistent right now, and where they might go on vacation together next summer.

"I ate too much," Claudia moaned when they'd finished. "But it was soooo good."

"Like you have to worry," Sally said, giving Claudia's figure an envious glance.

Claudia knew she was lucky. She seemed to have the kind of metabolism that allowed her to eat whatever she wanted without gaining weight, whereas poor Sally had to watch every bite religiously.

As she'd put it once, "Even the *smell* of carbohydrates causes my weight to shoot up two pounds!"

While their waiter calculated their bill, Claudia excused herself and headed for the ladies' room. As she rounded the corner leading to the restrooms, she was nearly knocked off her feet by a man walking fast in the opposite direction.

"Whoa, steady there," he said, grabbing her shoulders to keep her upright. "Sorry about that. I should have been looking where I was going."

Flustered, Claudia said, "You're right, you should have." Instantly sorry—after all, she was as much at fault as he was—she quickly amended, "Now *I'm* sorry. I wasn't watching, either." It was only then she really looked at him.

He was major cute. Major. Not handsome. Just cute, with a friendly, open face and dark eyes and thick, dark hair that was tousled and falling down on his forehead, and the *nicest* smile. *Wow,* Claudia thought. Now she really *was* flustered.

"Well," he said.

"Well," she said.

Then they both laughed.

"I—I was going to the ladies'." Claudia inwardly winced. *I was going to the ladies'.* What kind of stupid remark was *that?*

He grinned. "I just came from the mens'."

For the life of her, she couldn't think of another thing to say. So she stood there and wished she was clever and smart and had a snappy comeback the way cooler, cleverer, smarter women would have had. Finally, she realized she was staring at him and she could feel her face heating in embarrassment. She thanked all the gods in heaven that it was dimly lit back there because if he'd seen how she was blushing, she would have died. Just melted down into a puddle.

"Well, I'm sorry I wasn't looking," she said again. Oh, please. Could she *act* any dumber?

Clutching her handbag to her chest, she scurried off to the restroom without looking back.

Holy cow.

John Renzo felt as if he'd been slammed in his chest with a sledgehammer. Whoa, she was gorgeous. So gorgeous, he'd babbled like a thirteen-year-old confronted with his first big crush.

On a scale of one to ten, John would put her at about twenty. She was definitely the total package. Short blond spiky hair, huge blue eyes and a tall, slender body with curves in all the right places.

And that mouth!

Her lips were plump and pouty, just the kind he liked to kiss. John considered himself a connoisseur of lips. Hell, he'd practically majored in lips in college.

She looked like Meg Ryan.

Maybe she *was* Meg Ryan!

He laughed at his own idiocy. She was too young

to be Meg Ryan. He guessed her age at about twenty-eight. Thirty tops. Just right for his thirty-four.

He was still thinking about the perfect girl he'd nearly run down when he rejoined his buddies at their table.

"Hey, man, we thought you fell in!"

The joker was Matt Zelinsky, a videographer at the film production company where John worked.

"Ha ha," John said, pulling out his chair and joining the group. "You order yet?"

"Not yet." Jason Webb, a friend of Matt's who had recently become a regular part of their group, licked the salt from his margarita.

Just then, their waitress, a pretty young thing with wildly curly red hair, bounced over to their table. "Y'all ready to order?"

While the other three flirted with the waitress and placed their orders, John looked around the room to see if he could spy the Meg Ryan look-alike. Nope. He couldn't see her anywhere.

"Are you ready, sir?" the waitress said.

John grinned. "Sir? You think I'm a sir?"

She laughed. "I have to call everyone sir."

"Even girls?" John teased. Then, taking pity on her, he said, "I'll have the chicken quesadillas."

As he handed her the menu, he suddenly saw the blonde. She must have just returned from the rest room because she was in the process of sitting down at a table where a pretty brunette was already seated.

Listening to his buddies with half an ear, he covertly watched the blonde, all the while trying to figure out if he had nerve enough to approach her again. He had just about decided to get up and walk over when she and her friend stood, gathered their belongings and walked off.

Damn!

They were leaving!

"John. Hey, John. You deaf or something? I asked you a question."

John looked blankly at his friends, mumbled an apology, pushed back his chair and, ignoring their startled questions, took off after the blonde.

By the time he got to the front door, they'd already exited. John dashed out, looked left, then right. There they were, walking toward the parking lot. He reached them just as they climbed into a Jeep Wrangler—the blonde on the driver's side. Her eyes widened when she saw him.

"Don't be alarmed. I'm not a stalker." He grinned. "I *did* follow you out, though."

Now she smiled, too. "You did?"

Was it his imagination, or did she seem pleased?

"Yeah, I, uh…" Oh, hell. Might as well go for broke. "Look, I know you don't know me, but I'm a really nice guy. If you doubt it, my friends inside will all vouch for me."

Now the friend was smiling, too.

"Anyway, I wondered if I could call you sometime. Maybe we could catch a movie or even just meet for coffee."

Her smile turned regretful. "I'm sorry, but I don't think so."

John was surprised by how disappointed he felt.

"Thing is," she continued, "I don't live in Austin."

"Oh."

"I'm just visiting for the day."

He nodded. "Just my luck, I guess."

"But thanks. I...I'm flattered."

Still smiling, she turned the key in the ignition.

"Hey, wait," he said. Digging into his shirt pocket, he pulled out one of his business cards. He handed it to her. "If you come back and feel like it, that's my number."

She didn't say anything, but she did tuck the card into her purse. Then, with a wave, she drove off.

John stood and watched until the Jeep was out of sight, then, regretfully, he headed back inside the restaurant.

Chapter One

One month later…

"Y ou're breaking *up* with me?" Allison Carruthers, who had been John's girlfriend for the past year, stared at him in disbelief. "But I—I thought we were—" Her voice broke.

John knew what she'd thought. That one day they would probably get married. How could he explain without making the situation even worse than it was?

He wished he could explain how her anger and negativity had finally worn him down. But the one time he'd tried to talk to her about her tendency to expect the worst, she hadn't understood what he was talking about. She'd told him he was the one with the problem and that at least one person in a partnership had to be cautious and sensible.

Maybe if he loved her, he could have coped with that aspect of her personality. But the bottom line was, he had finally realized he wasn't in love with her.

"I'm sorry, Allison. I don't blame you for being upset. You deserve better." Why not try to leave her with her pride?

"I should have known this would happen. It's so typical. Men are so self-centered. I guess I didn't stroke your ego enough, right?"

John knew it was best to just ignore her gibe. "Look, I'll move my stuff out tomorrow."

She shook her head. Her face had become stony. "No. You'll move your stuff out *today.*"

John nodded. He'd wanted to make a clean break, but he'd been afraid it would have been adding insult to injury to dump the news that he wanted to sever their relationship, then immediately move his things out of her apartment.

He headed for the bedroom they'd shared for the past nine months. Opening the closet, he pulled down the suitcase he'd stored on the top shelf, then placed it on the unmade bed. Not wanting to take the time to fold his things properly, he pulled clothes off hangers and haphazardly tossed them into the open suitcase.

Next came the contents of the two drawers that held his underwear, socks and T-shirts. Soon it was obvious to him that the suitcase wasn't going to hold everything. *Damn.* He looked around. He needed some kind of big bag.

Remembering the garbage bags in the kitchen pantry, he headed in that direction. He stopped dead when he saw Allison. She was standing at the living room window with her back to him. Her shoulders shook. She was crying.

He swore to himself. He felt like a complete and total jerk. "Allison," he said softly, walking toward her. When he touched her shoulder, she twisted away.

"Don't touch me." Her voice was thick with tears.

Knowing the best thing he could do now was clear out of there fast, he left Allison and went into the kitchen for the garbage bags. Doubling two of them, he headed back to the bedroom and threw in the rest of his belongings. Once he was sure he had everything, he closed the suitcase. Removing the key to the apartment from his key chain, he placed it on the dresser. With the suitcase in one hand and the garbage bags in the other, he walked back out to the living area.

Allison still stood at the window. She turned around when she heard him. The tears were gone, but her face was blotchy. She was trying for an I-don't-give-a-damn look, but her eyes gave her away. It made John feel even worse to see the sadness in them. Despite everything, they'd shared a lot of good times together, and he hated that she was hurting.

"I'll call you, let you know where I'm staying, okay?" he said.

"Don't bother."

"Al…"

"Just go, John."

He sighed. The kindest thing he could do now was clear out fast. "Do you want me to write you a check now for what I think my share of this month's expenses will be?"

She bit her lip.

He knew she was torn between telling him to drop dead and the necessity to be practical. Setting his things down, he dug out his checkbook. Best to make it as easy as possible for her. He filled in a generous amount and placed the check on the coffee table.

"I left my key on the dresser," he said, picking up his bags again.

"Fine."

He hesitated. He had to say *something*. Finally, he settled for, "Take care, Al." Then, with a heavy heart, he quietly let himself out the door.

Claudia smiled as her Marketing 2255, Principles of Selling students noisily filed out of the classroom. When the last one had passed through the open doorway, she sat back in relief. Although she'd been teaching at Bayou City College for almost a month now, she still felt like a rank newbie. She wondered how long it would be before she felt like a real professor.

A real professor.

Professor Hathaway.

Every time one of her students called her Professor Hathaway, she wanted to laugh. It seemed so incredible that she was actually here. She was thrilled to have landed this job. Thrilled to be teaching in Houston and at such a fine college. Thrilled to be considered valuable on her own merits and not because she was a Hathaway.

Here at the college, no one even knew she was part of the Hathaway baking empire, and that was the way she wanted it to stay. Claudia needed to be judged for herself, not for her family's wealth and influence.

People who didn't have money thought those who did led a charmed life. Yes, it was nice not to have to worry about what things cost, to lead a comfortable, sheltered life, but there was a downside to that kind of wealth, too. You never knew if people liked you for yourself or because of what they imagined you could do for them.

Claudia knew firsthand what could happen. She had a couple of bad experiences behind her, and she didn't want to add another if she could help it. So she intended to keep her family background a secret as long as possible.

"Penny for your thoughts."

Claudia jumped. She'd been so lost in her thoughts she hadn't heard anyone enter. "Philip. Hi."

Philip Larkin, the CFO at the college, smiled down at her. "Got a few minutes?"

"Sure." From the hopeful expression on his face, Claudia knew Philip was probably going to ask her out again. On Monday, she'd finally said yes, and on Wednesday—today was Friday—they'd gone to an early movie after her last class, then stopped for pizza afterward.

She'd had a good time. Philip was very nice—a considerate, thoughtful date. He was nice-looking, too, with thick brown hair and blue eyes. On top of that, he actually listened to her instead of constantly talking about himself, the way so many guys seemed to do.

Despite everything in his favor, Claudia didn't know if she wanted to go out with Philip again. She'd been telling herself it was because she wasn't certain it was a good idea to date a colleague, especially one in the administrative end of the school.

But the truth was, Claudia felt no spark of attraction to Philip. It was a shame, too, because in addition to his other attributes, he was intelligent and obviously a really decent guy.

What's wrong with you? Do you think nice-looking, decent men with good jobs grow on trees?

She almost laughed at the thought, because it sounded so much like something her sisters would say. Her mother, of course, would want to know his pedigree.

"My cousin is turning thirty on Sunday," Philip said now. "She's invited some friends over to celebrate with her tomorrow night. I'd really like to take you to the party with me."

Claudia picked up a paper clip.

Philip sat on the edge of her desk. As always, he was dressed impeccably in spotless slacks, dress shirt and tie. Claudia knew he'd probably also worn a sport coat this morning, but imagined it was hanging in his office. "There'll be an interesting bunch of people there," he continued. "I think you'd enjoy meeting them. Jennifer—that's my cousin—works for one of the local TV stations here. She's a program coordinator—" He grinned. "She says that means she's in charge of all the grunt work."

Claudia turned the paper clip round and round in her hand. "Look, Philip, I'm really not good with lots of people I don't know—"

"I promise you. You'll enjoy it. Jen's brother is going to be there, too. John's a documentary film-maker. He's been working in Austin the past six years, but he's in the process of moving to Houston. He won't know most of the people there, either, so you won't be the only one."

"Oh, I don't know…"

"Come on. It'll be fun. You'll like these people, especially Jen. She's a sweetheart."

"Well…" Claudia decided she was being stupid. There weren't exactly dozens of guys lined up waiting to take her out. And after all, going out with Philip didn't mean she had to marry him. Besides, the party *did* sound like fun. "All right," she finally said. "You talked me into it."

"Great. I'll pick you up at seven."

Philip grinned all the way back to his office. *Yes!* She'd said yes. What he would have done if she'd continued to say no, he wasn't sure. All he knew was, where Claudia was concerned, he had no intention of giving up. Since Emily there had been no one he'd cared about, but that had all changed a month ago when Claudia had begun teaching at the college.

He'd known the moment he met her that she was special and that she was going to be important to him. He'd have felt foolish saying that to anyone, even John, but it was true. Philip had never believed in love at first sight, feeling that it took time to fall in love, that it was important to be friends first, that real love wasn't based on physical attraction but mutual interests and ideas.

Yet with Claudia, all those long-held beliefs flew out the window. It still amazed him that he could have fallen in love so quickly…and so hard.

He couldn't wait for John and Jen to meet her. It would be interesting to see what their reaction was. John, he knew, would see exactly what it was that had ensnared Philip so quickly, but women were different.

What if Jen didn't like Claudia? Would that make a difference?

Philip was so caught up in his thoughts, he jumped when Sarah Frost, his assistant, spoke to him.

"Sorry, I wasn't listening," he said.

"I said Dean Channing has called a meeting." Her dark eyes looked somber.

Philip frowned. "What's wrong?" But he was afraid he knew.

Sarah lowered her voice after first looking around to make sure no one else was in earshot. "I think it's about Professor Tate."

Philip swore under his breath. Just what he needed today. A week ago, Jeffrey Tate had been accused of sexual harassment by one of the sophomores. He swore he was innocent. The girl's parents were threatening to sue if Tate wasn't fired. But Philip knew Dean Channing was afraid Tate would sue if he *was*.

"All right," Philip said in resignation. "Print out all the information on Professor Tate's salary and benefits package, will you? I'd better be ready for anything when I get there."

All thoughts of Claudia were pushed from Philip's mind as he headed for his office.

* * *

After Philip went back to the administrative wing, Claudia began to clear off her desk. She had given a pop quiz in the form of an essay assignment to her Composition I class—much to their dismay—and she would have to read and grade the papers tonight. And she needed to read ahead for the Principles of Marketing class, which met tomorrow. And there was nothing in her condo to eat, which meant she'd better stop at the supermarket on the way home. She sighed. She'd better get a move on if she hoped to get everything done.

Claudia taught two classes of Composition I, which was a first-year course; one class of Composition II, a second-year course; two classes of Principles of Selling; and one class of Principles of Marketing—a total of 18 classroom hours a week. What with lesson planning, grading papers and tests, special projects and other related duties, it was a heavy load, especially for a first-year professor, but Claudia didn't mind. She loved teaching, particularly at this level. She'd found she had a natural rapport with her students, especially once they realized she had hands-on marketing experience herself.

With all her belongings packed into her tote, she slung her handbag over her shoulder and headed out to the parking lot. The late September heat blasted her when she exited the air-conditioned building. And when she unlocked the Jeep, it felt like an oven inside. After tossing her stuff into the back, she took off her brown linen jacket, exposing the white tank top she wore underneath.

With her favorite rock station blasting—and Claudia singing along in her slightly off-key voice—she edged the Jeep into Southwest Freeway traffic and headed south toward the Loop and her Galleria-area condo. Traffic was already heavy and it was only four o'clock on a Wednesday afternoon. But then, traffic always seemed to be heavy here.

Her family, most of whom lived in Morgan Creek, the small Texas town where Hathaway Baking had its main plant and offices, couldn't understand why she wanted to work somewhere like Houston, but Claudia loved the city. Yes, there were a lot of people. And yes, it was hot and humid for five months out of the year. And yes, the traffic could be horrendous.

But there was so much energy in the city. It was exciting. There was a feeling here that anything could be accomplished if you just worked hard enough. And the shopping, the theater and arts scene, the restaurants and the museums were fabulous.

Claudia loved it all. There was nothing about Morgan Creek she missed except her siblings and her nieces. But a person couldn't have everything. Sometimes you had to choose, and she'd chosen to cut the cord that she'd felt slowly strangling her.

She had managed to spend a few hours in Morgan Creek last Sunday, and that was nice. She'd enjoyed talking to Bryce and Lorna, telling them about her new job and hearing about everything that had happened since she'd left. It had been nice to see how happy Bryce was now, too, married to Amy—who had been nanny to his two young daughters—and father to her little girl. Bryce certainly deserved to be happy, Claudia thought, after suffering through so much pain when he lost his first wife, whom he'd loved so dearly.

Claudia had spent Saturday afternoon and evening with Sally in Austin, and that had been fun, too. All in all, it was a good weekend, even though not everything had worked out the way she'd hoped. One of the reasons she'd made the trip home so soon after moving to Houston was that she'd been unable to get the cute guy she'd met that day in August out of her mind. She'd kept thinking about him and finally she'd decided she would call him when she got to Sally's, see if he wanted to go to a party they were invited to attend that night.

Remembering how she'd felt when she'd called the number on the card she'd gotten from him, Claudia frowned. She'd been so sure Jason Webb liked her. That he'd meant it when he'd given her his business card and asked her to call him the next time she was in Austin.

But Jason Webb didn't remember her. In fact, he

seemed to have no idea who she was, even after she'd mentioned the restaurant where they'd literally bumped into one another. He said he was sorry, but he didn't remember meeting her. Claudia was so embarrassed, she didn't elaborate or try to explain. She just said she was sorry to have bothered him and hung up. It wasn't meant to be, she told herself afterward, furious with herself for being a romantic fool.

Deliberately, she had put him out of her mind, but obviously that hadn't worked, for here she was, thinking about him again.

"Stop that," she muttered. "You'll never see Jason Webb again, and even if you did, you probably wouldn't like him."

Seeing the entrance to the supermarket, she put on her turn signal and all thoughts of Jason Webb were finally wiped from her mind as she mentally began to form her shopping list.

John made good time driving into Houston from Austin. He had mixed emotions about his company's relocating. On the one hand, he hated leaving Austin— a city he loved. On the other, he was looking forward to living close to his family again, especially his sister and his cousin, Philip—who also happened to be his best friend. Not to mention the man who had saved his life.

John knew if he lived to be a hundred, he could

never repay Philip who—three years ago, without a moment's hesitation—had agreed to give John one of his kidneys after both John's kidneys failed as a result of the damage caused by a severe case of nephritis when he was ten.

Which reminded John—he should call Philip, let him know he was on his way in. Whipping out his cell phone, he punched five. Speed dial kicked in and moments later, Philip answered.

"Hey, cuz," John said. "I'm headin' into town. Just left Prairie View." He glanced at the clock on his dashboard. "I should get to Jen's about two."

"Oh, you're going straight there?"

"Yeah, I told her I'd help her get ready for tonight. I guess she's expecting a bunch of people."

"About thirty, she said."

"You still cool about me bunking with you until I find a place?"

"Sure. No problem."

"Why don't you come over to Jen's early, too?"

"I would, but I'm bringing a date tonight, and I told her I'd pick her up at seven."

There was something in Philip's voice that made John smile. "So who's the date? Anybody I know?"

"It's that new prof I told you about. The one I've been trying to get to go out with me for weeks."

"So you finally wore her down, huh?"

"Actually, I took her to a movie Wednesday night."

John could almost hear the smile in his cousin's voice. "I can't wait to meet her."

"Just remember. I saw her first."

"She's that hot?" John teased. He laughed when Philip sputtered something about her being a nice girl. "Nice girls can be hot, too." Then he took pity on his cousin. "Tell me about her. What's she look like?"

"I'd rather wait and just let you see for yourself."

"Not even a hint?"

Before Philip could answer, John saw flashing lights ahead of him. "I'd better hang up. There're cops up ahead."

"Okay, see you tonight."

Vehicles slowed as drivers rubbernecked the fender bender that had brought the cops out, but once past the scene, traffic quickly resumed speed. As John covered the final miles to his sister's place, he thought about his cousin and the girl he was bringing to the party tonight. He was glad the elusive Claudia had finally said yes to Phil, who had not had good luck with women.

In fact, since Emily had broken their engagement— jeez, was it already three years since she'd taken that job in London?—Phil hadn't been seriously interested in anyone. John had begun to think he'd never get over Emily, so when he'd started talking about how much he liked this new prof they'd hired, John had been happy for his cousin and had hoped the girl would like Phil, too.

Funny how a guy could go along for years never meeting anyone who interested him, then *wham,* along came the perfect girl. John grimaced. *He'd* met the perfect girl, too. In fact, meeting her had been the catalyst that had finally forced him to face and do something about the situation with Allison. Unfortunately, he'd made a major mistake in not finding out who the girl was and how to get in touch with her.

Instead, he'd given her one of his business cards, hoping she'd call *him.* And she hadn't. He was still kicking himself for goofing up so badly, because although their meeting had been brief, John knew he wasn't likely to meet anyone even remotely like her again.

Nope. Opportunity had knocked and he hadn't answered. He wouldn't get a second chance.

Claudia couldn't decide what to wear. Why hadn't she asked Philip if the party was casual or dressy? She wondered if she should try to call him and find out.

Finally she settled on an outfit that could go either way—a long, black jersey skirt with a slit up the back, black chunky mules and a black tank top. Around her neck she looped a long gray, fringed scarf. Digging around in her jewelry box, she found some black hoop earrings. Four black and silver bracelets came next. Claudia was from the school of thought that believed if one bracelet was good, four was better.

Looking at her unpainted nails, she wished she'd taken the time to get a manicure, but it was too late now. She would have to do in her unvarnished state.

Her doorbell rang at precisely seven. She smiled. She had known Philip would be punctual. All she'd had to do was take one look at his neat, everything-in-its-place office to know he believed in order. Most of the time, Claudia did, too, so that was fine.

She opened the door. "Hi."

"Hi." His gaze took her in. "Wow. You look great."

"Thanks." He was his usual well-dressed self in neat khakis, a dark blue knit shirt and shiny brown loafers. Claudia grabbed her sack purse from the little table next to the door. "I'm ready."

As they walked down the path to the visitor parking lot, Philip said, "This is a nice area."

"Yes, I think so."

"The rent must be high, though."

Claudia wasn't renting. She'd bought her condo, but she knew if she said so, he'd wonder how she could afford it. She thought fast. "Actually, my grandmother left me a little money, and I figured real estate would give me a better return than the stock market."

"That was very smart."

"I can't take all the credit. My brother helped me come to that decision."

"Older brother?"

"Yes."

"So you have a brother? Are there just the two of you?"

"Um, no. I, uh, have two older sisters." By now they were underway, heading east on Potomac toward Westheimer.

"You're lucky. I'm an only. But I told you that the other night, didn't I?"

There had been times Claudia had wished she were an only child, too. But now she knew Philip was right. She *was* lucky. Especially since her siblings were all people she would choose as friends if they weren't related to her. Her parents were a different story.

"I guess that's why I've been so close to Jen and John," Philip continued. "Or maybe it's because we're double cousins."

"Double cousins?"

"Yeah. My mother is John's father's sister. And *his* mother is *my* father's sister."

"*Really?* Who married first?"

"John's mom—my aunt Linda—and his dad Lou got married first. Then my dad met my uncle Lou's sister Margie—my mom—and two years later they got married. John is two years older than me."

"So I guess your two families get along really well."

"Best friends all around." He smiled. "I've never heard one cross word between them."

"Now *you're* the lucky one."

"Oh? Your family *doesn't* get along?"

Claudia shrugged. She didn't want to get into her family's dynamics. Couldn't if she hoped to keep the Hathaway Baking connection a secret. "It's just normal stuff. Dad drinks too much. Mom is controlling. That kind of thing."

Philip obviously sensed her reluctance to say more for soon after he changed the subject. They were deep into the respective talents of Sheryl Crow versus Shania Twain when Philip pulled up in front of a small bungalow in an area he identified as the outskirts of River Oaks. "I don't know if you know anything about River Oaks?"

"Just that it's a really high-rent district."

"Yeah, it is. Jen doesn't own this place, though. She and a girlfriend—a co-worker, actually—rent the house."

There were already a dozen or more cars parked along the street. Philip pulled into the driveway, saying, "Family has its privileges."

"Will your parents be here tonight?"

"No. We're doing the family thing tomorrow at Jen's parents' house. Tomorrow is actually her birthday."

"So both families live here in Houston?"

"Yep. Native Houstonians all."

As they walked up onto the small front stoop, Claudia could hear laughter and music inside. Philip rang the doorbell, then without waiting for someone to answer, opened the door and gestured her inside.

A pretty dark-haired young woman in a red sundress that showed off a golden tan walked toward them. She smiled at Philip. "Hey, cuz, you made it."

"Happy birthday, Jen." Philip leaned down and kissed her cheek.

"Thanks." Her dark-eyed gaze moved curiously to Claudia. "Hi. I'm Jennifer, Philip's cousin." She extended her hand.

"Hi, Jennifer. I'm Claudia. Claudia Hathaway." They shook hands.

"I'm glad you could come." Jennifer's smile was warm and friendly.

Claudia knew instantly she would like this woman. Suddenly she was very glad she'd accepted Philip's invitation. "Me, too."

Claudia and Philip followed Jennifer into the living room were several groups of young people stood talking. In rapid succession Jennifer introduced them in a blur of names Claudia knew she wouldn't remember. Most seemed to be Jennifer's co-workers at the TV station.

"Where's John?" Philip asked Jennifer when she'd finished with the introductions.

"Out back, I think."

"Come on, Claudia. Let's go out. I want you to meet John."

Giving Jennifer a smile, Claudia let herself be led through the house and out the back door where several young men stood drinking beer.

"There you are!" Philip said.

The men turned around.

Claudia stared in disbelief.

For walking toward them with a huge smile on his face was none other than Jason Webb.

Chapter Two

John couldn't believe his eyes. Philip's date was the blonde! The one John had met in Austin.

She'd recognized him, too. He could see the surprise in her eyes.

"John," Philip was saying. "Hey, man, it's good to see you." John returned Philip's hug, but all the while, his mind was spinning.

Releasing John, Philip proudly drew the blonde forward. "John, this is Claudia Hathaway, the new prof I was telling you about. Claudia, my cousin, John Renzo."

She tilted her head, studying John. "Actually, I believe we've met."

"You've met?" Philip looked from one to the other.

"Yeah," John said, nodding agreement. "You're right. We *have* met."

Now Philip was frowning. "But you never said anything."

John shrugged. "I didn't know her name." He couldn't stop staring at her. God, she was even more gorgeous than he'd remembered. Tonight, in that black clingy outfit, she looked fantastic. Although she was lean, her body was sexy, with curves in the right places. And *she* was the wonderful Claudia that Philip had been talking about for weeks? How was that possible?

Philip gave Claudia a puzzled smile. "How did you two meet?"

"We kind of bumped into each other. At a restaurant in Austin one weekend when I went in to meet Sally. I told you about Sally—my college roommate?"

"I nearly knocked Claudia over," John said. "I wasn't looking where I was going."

Philip smiled. "Typical." Turning to Claudia, he added, "John's always been accident-prone. As a kid, he kept falling out of trees or running into walls."

John grinned. "Hey, I was adventurous. I liked to take chances." He still couldn't get over the fact that the girl he'd thought about so many times over the past month was actually standing there. In the flesh. In the *gorgeous* flesh.

"That's true," Philip conceded, "I'm a much more careful sort. I prefer not to take unnecessary risks."

"Which is why you have the kind of job you do, and I have the kind of job I do," John said.

"I'm afraid I'm more like John," Claudia said. "When I was little, I always had a black-and-blue mark or a scab somewhere."

"Then I balance you out perfectly," Philip said happily, putting a possessive arm around Claudia.

John knew the hot stab of jealousy he felt was beneath him. He should be glad for Philip. Claudia was the kind of girl any man would love to claim, and if she liked Philip, then good for him. But even as he told himself this, he wished he could trade places with his cousin. He wished it more than he'd wished anything in a long time.

"Hey, you two, quit monopolizing Claudia."

All three turned at the sound of Jennifer's voice. "Claudia," she said, "come with me. Some other guests have arrived that I'd like you to meet. Anyway, once these two get together, they forget anyone else is around. Let's let them talk for a while."

"All right." With a little wave goodbye, Claudia followed Jennifer into the house.

Once they were gone, Philip said, "What's the *real* story here?"

"What do you mean, real story?"

"You know. The real story about what happened between you and Claudia."

"Nothing happened."

"Yet you remembered her, and she remembered you."

"Wouldn't *you* remember her if you'd met her casually? Hell, she's gorgeous. Besides, one of the guys I was with mentioned how she kind of resembles Meg Ryan. That really planted her in my mind."

"I'm surprised you didn't ask her out."

"Maybe I did." Seeing the look on Philip's face, John laughed. "Don't worry. She said no."

Philip grinned. "Shows she's got good sense." He walked over to the cooler where the beer was iced down and removed a can. Popping the top, he took a long drink.

"Yeah," John said, "she obviously realized you're a much more upstanding citizen than me."

For a while after that, they talked about John's new job in Houston, but Philip seemed antsy, and John knew his cousin wanted to go back inside and find Claudia. John didn't blame him. If she was John's date, he wouldn't leave her alone for a minute.

For the next hour or so, John stayed away from Philip and Claudia. He busied himself talking to the other people. But he kept watching for a chance to talk to Claudia alone. About nine-thirty, he spotted her sitting by herself on the window seat in the dining room. Philip was nowhere in sight. John quickly walked over.

"Mind if I join you?"

She smiled. "No." She scooted over.

He sat down beside her. "It's good to see you again."

"You, too."

She had a disconcerting way of looking directly into his eyes. "Small world, huh?"

"Yes, it is."

For a brief moment, John felt awkward. But he pressed on. "So. Were you living here in Houston that day we met?"

She shook her head. "Uh-uh. I moved here the first of September…when I started my job at the college."

Boy, he liked her voice. It was low and musical. Sexy. *Oh, come on! Who do you think you're kidding? You like everything about her!* "Where'd you move from?"

"A little town south of Austin."

"Were you a teacher there?"

"No. This is my first teaching job."

"Do you like it?"

"So far I love it."

"I moved to Houston to take a new job, too."

"Philip said you're a filmmaker."

"Yeah."

"What kind of films?"

"All kinds. Documentaries. Advertising films. Training films. You name it, we do it."

"Are you a cameraman? Is that the right term?"

He grinned. "No. And no. Producing and directing is my area of expertise. And the correct terminology is camera operator or videographer. But we're loose. We answer to just about anything."

For a moment she fell silent, and as casually as he could manage, he said, "You know, after I met you that day? I kind of hoped I'd hear from you again."

"Oh, really?"

Something about the way she'd responded struck him as odd. "Yeah. I was disappointed when I didn't. In fact, I was kind of kicking myself for not finding out your name so I could call *you*."

She seemed to consider that for a moment. Then, blue eyes meeting his, she said, "I *did* try to call you."

"You *did?*"

"Yes."

"When?"

"Last weekend, actually. I was in Austin for the day and thought I'd invite you to a party some friends were giving."

"But…did you call my cell phone number?"

She shrugged. "I called whatever number was on that card you gave me."

"That's my cell phone." He couldn't believe he'd missed her call. "I don't remember getting a missed message signal."

"That's because someone answered the phone."

"Somebody else answered my *cell* phone?" Now

John was thoroughly confused. How was that possible? His cell phone never left his possession. "Maybe you misdialed."

"I didn't misdial."

"I don't understand."

"There's something I don't understand, either. Why did you tell me your name was Jason Webb?"

"Jason Webb?" Something was totally screwy here. "Jason is a friend of mine. Why would you think *I* was Jason?"

"That's what it said on the card you gave me."

John stared at her. Then he swore. "I'm an idiot!" He realized he must have mistakenly pulled out the card Jason had given him earlier that day instead of his own. "I gave you the wrong card. Jason was one of the guys I was having lunch with that day, and he had some new business cards he passed out. I must have stuck his in the pocket where I keep some of mine."

"Ah," she said. "That explains it."

"So you talked to Jason?"

She smiled. "Yes."

"What did he say?"

"Well, he obviously had no idea who I was, and I was too embarrassed to try to explain. See, the thing is, I thought it was you I was talking to…and that you didn't remember me."

John wanted to say there was no way he could have ever forgotten her, but he stopped himself just in time.

No matter how much he liked this girl, she was Philip's date. John had no right to undercut him. Nor did he want to.

But he couldn't help wondering what might have happened if he'd given her the right card. Would she still have come here with Philip? Or would she be John's date tonight?

Yet what difference did it make now? Even if she encouraged him, there was nothing he could do to change things. She *was* here with Philip, and he knew Philip was already halfway in love with her. Unless his cousin decided he was no longer interested in her, John could do nothing but sit on the sidelines.

And keep kicking himself.

"Are you having a good time?"

Claudia smiled at Jennifer. "Yes, I am. You have nice friends."

"Thank you."

"And the food is great. Did you make it all yourself?"

"Uh-huh. I love to cook and bake. If I wasn't in the communications field, I would've gone to culinary school." She made a face. "Some days I really wish I had."

"I was like that all the years I worked in sales. Last year I finally decided I had to make some changes in my life or go nuts. So I picked up the last few graduate hours I needed and started applying for jobs, and now…here I am."

Jennifer studied her gravely. "I have a feeling you're braver than I am."

"Oh, I doubt that. You probably just haven't reached the point where you're ready to make a change. Maybe you never will. I mean, I'm sure people in all professions get frustrated at times."

Jennifer nodded. "Yes, you're probably right. I know my dad complains about his work a lot, and so has John. In fact, he just changed companies."

"He did mention that."

"Yeah, the company he worked for in Austin wasn't getting the kinds of projects he hoped to work on. So he started looking around a month or so ago and ended up landing a job with a really successful film company here. He's thrilled." She smiled. "So am I. I missed him when he lived in Austin. Now all my family is right here in Houston, and that's the way I like it."

"Philip was telling me about your family on the way over. How you and he are double cousins."

"Yes, it's kind of neat. Our parents are really close. Thank goodness. It would be awful if they didn't get along. I feel so sorry for people whose families are constantly fighting."

"Me, too," Claudia said fervently.

"Philip told me you have a couple of sisters and a brother?"

"Yes."

Jennifer seemed to hesitate, then said, "Phil really likes you."

Claudia didn't know what to say. Involuntarily, her gaze moved past Jennifer to John, who stood nearby talking to a cute redhead. When he laughed and touched the redhead's arm, Claudia jerked her gaze away. "Philip is very nice."

Jennifer studied her thoughtfully. "Yes, he is. Have you two been dating long?"

Claudia shook her head. "This is only the second time I've been out with him."

"Really? I thought—" Jennifer broke off. "Obviously, I misunderstood."

Claudia would have liked to pursue this statement, but just then, Philip walked up to them. "I hope you're telling Claudia what a great guy I am," he said to Jennifer.

She laughed. "Oh, you men. You're impossible. You think the entire world revolves around you, don't you?"

"You mean it doesn't?" This came from John, who had also walked up behind them. He put his arm companionably around Philip's shoulders.

Jennifer rolled her eyes.

Claudia laughed.

"Now where were we?" Jennifer said to Claudia.

"You were telling her what a great guy I am," Philip said, grinning.

"On that note, I think I'd better check on the food," Jennifer said. "Last time I looked, the potato casserole was fast disappearing." She was laughing as she walked away.

"I guess that's my cue to leave, too," John said. But he didn't look as if he wanted to go.

For a moment, no one spoke. Because of the silence between them, Claudia became aware of the music playing. It was an old rock tune, one of her favorites. "Now's your chance to impress me, Philip. I'd love to dance."

"Me?" He gave her a look of mock horror. "I have two left feet. But John's a good dancer." He turned to John. "Can I trust you with her?"

Claudia's heart did a little skip as John's gaze met hers. "Of course you can, said the big bad wolf," John answered in a deep voice.

All three laughed and John took her arm, leading her out to the small area that had been cleared for dancing.

Claudia soon discovered John was a great dancer. He had a loose body with a natural rhythm that couldn't be taught. Claudia loved to dance, so when "Proud Mary" wound up and the next song was a slow ballad, she allowed herself to be drawn into his arms for that one, too.

"Having a good time?" he asked.

He was wearing some kind of woodsy scent—aftershave or cologne—she couldn't tell which. Whatever it was, she liked it. "Yes, I am."

He pulled her just a fraction closer. "Me, too."

Claudia closed her eyes. She had a feeling it might be a mistake to indulge in any fantasies about John, but she couldn't seem to help herself.

Why didn't you give me the right business card?

She was acutely aware of their bodies touching. No wonder some religions banned the activity. Dancing had to be one of the sexiest things two people could do.

She forced herself to smile brightly when the song ended. "Thanks. I enjoyed that."

Philip was waiting right where they'd left him. He reached for her hand. "That's enough. I want her now."

"I don't blame you," John said lightly. He bowed to Claudia. "Thank you, ma'am." Then, with a little salute, he headed off in the direction of the kitchen.

For the remainder of the evening, Claudia didn't see much of him. He was either outside or in another room, and she decided that was for the best. Whatever might have been if they'd been able to connect seemed to be a closed chapter.

It was probably best to put him out of her mind for good.

On the way home, Philip was in a talkative mood. "So what did you think of John and Jen?"

"I liked them both a lot."

"And they liked you." He smiled. "Jennifer said she thought you were terrific."

"I think she and I could be friends." And John...was it foolish to think they could be something more than friends?

"She's a really nice person. I wish something good would happen for her the way it has for me." He reached over and squeezed her hand for a moment.

Claudia knew he was referring to meeting her, and that made her uncomfortable. Yet she couldn't think of anything to say without making too big a deal out of his comment. "Why? Did something bad happen to her?"

He didn't answer for a moment. When he did, his voice had sobered. "Two years ago her fiancé was killed. He was an Air Force pilot whose helicopter was shot down in Iraq only days before he was supposed to be sent home."

"Oh, God, how terrible."

"Yeah, it was. She had a really rough time. She's still not over it."

"That's just awful. Is she dating at all?"

"Not that I know of."

She waited a few moments before saying, "What about...John? I take it he's not involved with anyone, either."

"Nope, not now. He *was* seeing somebody pretty

steady. In fact, they were living together. Everyone thought he was finally ready to make a commitment, but they broke up in August."

"Oh?" August was when Claudia met John. "What happened?"

"All he said was that something made him realize he wasn't in love with Allison. So he broke it off."

Claudia told herself she was indulging in a romantic fantasy to even consider that John might have been referring to meeting her when he said something had happened to cause him to break off his relationship.

You sure have a high opinion of yourself, don't you? Men like John do not break off long-term relationships because they exchange a couple of words with you! Then again, she had no idea what John was really like, now did she?

"Jen and her mother were both glad when they broke up," Philip continued.

"Why's that? Didn't they like Allison?"

"They both thought Allison was too negative and moody." He laughed. "But I think those two feel no one is good enough for John."

Claudia wanted to keep asking him questions about John, but they had just pulled up in front of Claudia's condominium complex, so her window of opportunity was over.

"Thanks for inviting me to the party," Claudia said when they reached her door. "I had a really nice time." Opening her purse, she withdrew her keys.

"I'm glad," he said. "I did, too."

She unlocked the door. "Well, good night, Philip."

"Good night, Claudia." And then, before she could avoid it, he leaned over and kissed her. Unless she wanted to make a huge thing out of it, she couldn't pull away. So she closed her eyes and pretended it was John kissing her. Even that didn't help. There were just no fireworks, at least for her. Gently, she broke the kiss before it could go on too long. The last thing she wanted to do was send the wrong message.

"I'd better go in," she said. "It's late." Because she felt she sounded too abrupt, she smiled. "See you Monday."

If he'd been like some of the guys she'd dated in the past, he would have tried to change her mind, but Philip obviously wasn't that kind of person, because all he said was, "Sweet dreams," and then he turned and walked away.

Inside, Claudia leaned against the closed door gratefully. She hated dating. There ought to be some kind of test you could give a person that would tell you if he was someone you'd want to go out with more than once. Some kind of magic word you could say, and if he didn't give you the right answer back, you'd know he wasn't for you.

Oh, sure, just like bad things should only happen to bad people....

Laughing at herself, she turned out the hall light and headed for bed.

Philip couldn't stop thinking about how it had felt to kiss Claudia. He'd wanted to deepen the kiss, but he was afraid to push. She hadn't seemed ready, and he didn't want to blow his chances with her just because he was greedy for more than she was willing to give.

She was wonderful.

So different from Emily.

Maybe that was part of the reason he liked Claudia so much, because she *was* so different. Normally Philip didn't allow himself to dwell on Emily and the way she'd dumped him, but tonight the memories didn't hurt. That was Claudia's doing. Now that he'd met her and knew he could really care for her, he was glad Emily had showed her true colors before they'd gotten married.

He should have seen the breakup coming because Emily had made no bones about her ambition. A financial analyst with one of the big oil companies, she couldn't understand why he was content to work for a small college. She'd kept pushing him to look for another job, one that paid better and had more prestige.

"There's nowhere for you to go there, Philip," she'd said more than once.

He'd tried to explain that he liked the small college venue. That he didn't want a high-stress job. That there was more to life than making lots of money. He guessed he'd blinded himself to the fact that she'd never agreed with him, so when she'd told him she'd gotten a "stupendous" job offer in London and intended to take it, he'd been stunned.

Philip wasn't like John. John attracted women like flypaper attracts flies. Philip knew why. John was outgoing and fun and he had a job women found glamorous. Philip was much quieter and cautious, and his job sounded dull to other people.

But Claudia…Claudia was different.

She was a teacher. Obviously, money and glamour were not important to her or she'd be in another profession.

And when John had asked her out, she'd said no. Philip smiled over that one.

That fact alone would have told him he'd met the right woman for him.

Chapter Three

"You'll never guess who was at the party last night!"

"If you say Johnny Depp, I'll have to kill you."

Claudia laughed. Sally was currently wildly in love with Johnny Depp. "No, Sally, not Johnny Depp."

"Well, that's a relief! Who, then?"

"You know that cute guy? The one I met in August?"

"The one you called last weekend that didn't remember you, you mean?"

"Yes, that one."

"*He* was at the party?"

"Uh-huh. He's Philip's cousin!"

"You're kidding."

"And guess what else?"

"There's more?"

Claudia explained about the mix-up with the business card and how John wasn't Jason Webb but John Renzo. "Sally, he's going to be living here. He's taken a job in Houston."

"What're you going to do?" Sally said when Claudia had finished.

"What *can* I do?"

"I know you really liked him. Do you think you'll go out with him?"

"I don't think that's in the cards."

"Because of his cousin?"

Claudia sighed. "Yes. They're really tight. So even if he still wanted to, I doubt John will ask me out."

"How do you feel about that?"

"I don't know. Right now I'm totally confused."

"Aside from seeing John at the party, how'd it go?"

"It was fun. I had a good time. Everyone there was really nice. And Jennifer and I really hit it off. I think we could be good friends. If only…" But what was the use of wishing? It wasn't as if wishes would change anything.

"If only what?"

Claudia sighed again, more deeply this time. "I just wish things would work out the way they're supposed to once in a while." She remembered how she'd felt when she and John were dancing. "I mean, I think I could really like John. There's a real chemistry between us. But now that I've gone out with Philip, and I know *he* really likes me, everything is totally screwed up. John won't want to step on Philip's toes and Philip wants to see me again. Oh, shoot. I don't know what to do."

"Did Philip kiss you good-night?"

"Yes."

"And?"

"And nothing. The kiss was pleasant, but that's it. There was absolutely no zing."

Sally was silent for a few seconds. Then she sighed, too. "Why does life have to be so complicated?"

Claudia laughed. "Is that a rhetorical question?"

After they hung up, Claudia sat there pensively for a long time. She kept going over and over everything that had happened the previous evening. The things John had said and not said. The things Philip had said and not said. And the things she had said and not said.

Finally she came to a decision. It wouldn't matter how many times she went out with Philip. She would never feel any differently toward him. She liked him as a friend and hoped she could keep him as a friend. But there was simply no chemistry between them at all, at least not on her part, and there never would be.

So when he asked her out again—and he *would,* of that, she had no doubt—she would turn him down.

She would be kind and let him down gently.

And who knew? Maybe Philip would find someone else to date. And then she and John...

Claudia let the thought trail off, afraid to hope.

John spent Monday morning getting brought up to speed on the current working projects at Buffalo Films, his new employer. He'd toured the facility when he'd interviewed, but Kurt Kenyon, who was the owner's right-hand man and in effect managed the day-to-day operation of the company, gave him a more in-depth tour and introduced him to all the employees who were working in-house that day.

Soon John's head was swimming with names. Buffalo had about sixty employees, and at least forty of them were there that morning. John knew it would take a while before he could put names to faces, but he made an effort to at least retain the names of the art director and the acquisitions director.

After the tour, Kurt showed John into a small office that contained a no-nonsense metal desk, a four-drawer filing cabinet, a computer and printer, and two chairs—one behind the desk, one off to the side.

"Right now, this'll be your office," Kurt said. "When a bigger one becomes available, we'll move you."

"This is fine," John said. He didn't expect to be in his office much anyway.

Kurt nodded. "Ready to dive in?"

"More than ready."

"Good. I've got a special project for you. In fact, the only reason we got the project was because these people heard you were coming on board."

John was pleased to know his reputation had preceded him. "Who is it?"

"The Fairchild Cancer Center. They've contracted for a promo video with the proviso that you'll direct."

"No kidding? But I thought they had their own media department."

"They're trying to cut costs and have decided the media department is going. Guess it'll be cheaper for them to contract out."

"What kind of promo video?"

"They're working on an experimental treatment for certain types of cancer and they want us to follow one of the patients who's participating. A start-to-finish kind of thing."

"How're they planning to use the promotion?"

"It'll be sent to hospitals and cancer specialists around the world as well as shown on various health channels."

"Budget?"

Kurt named a figure.

John's eyes widened. At least they seemed willing to spend enough to put out a high-quality product.

"Richard Philbin, their public relations manager, wants to meet with you this afternoon."

"How much of a crew can I have?"

"A videographer—I'm thinking Paul, you met him earlier, he's the one with the shaved head, a PA—Laurie's the best one we've got, and an audio tech—probably Doug. They're a good crew. They've worked on several projects together. You saw one of them. That Larrimer spot? You know, the dancers?"

John nodded, pleased he'd have a production assistant. That would take a whole load of crap off his shoulders.

"Okay. Here's Philbin's number." Kurt handed John a business card. "Give him a call. We'll either talk today after you've met with him or tomorrow morning if your meeting runs late. By the way, Susan ordered some business cards for you. We should have them tomorrow."

John didn't reach Richard Philbin on the first try and had to leave a message. But Philbin returned his call within the hour and they agreed to meet at three that afternoon in Philbin's office.

Since John hadn't anticipated a client meeting, he hadn't dressed for one that morning. So at noon, instead of going out for Thai food with some of the guys, he headed for Philip's town house where he changed into black dress slacks, a black shirt and gray tie—his official look.

John arrived at Fairchild fifteen minutes before he was due. Luckily, Philbin's earlier appointment finished ahead of time, so John only had to wait ten minutes before being ushered into Philbin's nicely furnished tenth-floor office in the middle of the medical center area.

Philbin turned out to be a handsome gray-haired man of about fifty. He gave John a quick once-over and seemed to approve. After handshakes and an offer of coffee or a Coke, Philbin got right down to business. "What I'm looking for," he said, leaning back in his chair, "is a video that seems more human interest than self-serving promotion. You know, the kind of thing *Dateline* or *60 Minutes* would do." He smiled. "Is that possible?"

"Sure. You just tell me what you want, and I'll find a way to do it."

"Good."

"But first, fill me in on the patient."

"His name is Travis Feeney. He's seventeen, an athlete. Plays baseball for Bayou Bend High School. Last season he was their star pitcher and they went on to win State in their division. He was being touted as someone who might end up getting drafted for one of the pro teams. Those days, however, are probably over."

John shook his head. Seventeen. Life sure as hell wasn't fair. "What kind of cancer does he have?"

"A brain tumor, much of which was removed by surgery. What couldn't be removed is now being treated with chemotherapy and radiation."

"I thought this was some kind of experimental program you're pushing."

"It is. What's experimental are the drugs themselves, which are new and which are being used in more concentrated amounts than normal. Travis is nearly finished with the program, and we have high hopes that all traces of his cancer will be gone by the end. His last couple of MRIs have shown a steady decrease in cancer cells."

"If that's the case, why would you say his baseball days are over?" Noticing Philbin's frown, John hurriedly added, "I'm not questioning you because I doubt what you're saying. I need to know so that I can understand the situation from all angles. That'll help in the creative planning." He could see Philbin relax at his explanation.

They continued talking for the better part of an hour. Philbin then took John on a tour of the section where Travis Feeney's treatment was taking place. John was introduced to Travis's oncologist and the team of nurses and doctors involved in his treatment program.

"Tomorrow morning I'd like to take you to meet Travis," Philbin said when they were finished. "You can see where he lives, meet his parents and sister. Afterwards, we can go by the school. His coach has agreed to talk to you, too."

By the time John left Philbin, his mind was already

churning with ideas, and he knew many more would come once he'd had a chance to meet Travis Feeney and see him in his home setting. He was excited about this project. It wouldn't be the most ambitious he'd ever tackled, but it would be among the more interesting. It would also be prestigious—a nice addition to his résumé.

By the time he got back to Buffalo Films, it was after five. Kurt was still there doing some editing, but when he saw John, he stopped, and they sat and talked for an hour and a half. John gave Kurt a rundown of the meeting and some of his ideas for what he might aim for in the finished video. Kurt threw out some ideas of his own, and it turned into a good brainstorming session.

Finally Kurt looked at his watch. It was almost seven. "I'm starved. Want to go grab some Mexican food?"

"Sounds good."

John enjoyed the meal and Kurt's company. Later, as he drove home and thought about the day, he knew he'd made the right choice in taking this job in Houston. Already, he was more energized and excited than he'd been in a long time.

In fact, life would be just about perfect if only *he* was the one dating Claudia Hathaway instead of Philip. The moment the thought popped into his head, he felt guilty.

Jesus, he had to stop *thinking* about her.

Unfortunately, he'd been telling himself this since the party on Saturday, and he hadn't been successful following it yet.

Take yesterday.

In the middle of Sunday dinner at his parents' house, thoughts of Claudia kept creeping in and causing him to lose track of the conversation. It got so bad at one point that his father had said, "What's wrong with you today, John? You seem a million miles away."

John started. "I'm sorry. I was just thinking about the new job. Nervous, I guess."

His father peered at him over his glasses. "You? I didn't think anything made you nervous."

John forced a laugh that sounded fake even to him. "Oh, c'mon, Dad. I'm not that conceited."

"I don't think that's what your dad meant," John's mother Linda chimed in. "It's more that you're so confident." She turned to John's father. "Isn't that right, Lou?"

His dad, who had just taken a bite of his pasta, nodded. But he was still looking at John in a thoughtful way.

"Mom nailed it," Jen said. "Sometimes to the point that we mortals who *aren't* always confident would like to choke you."

"I wouldn't go that far," Linda said. But she laughed.

"I would," Jen retorted, elbowing John in the process.

"Hey, who asked *you?*" John said, but he laughed, too, and thankfully, the subject was dropped.

Remembering, John grimaced. If his family had known what—*whom*—he was thinking about and what those thoughts were, they would have been disappointed in him. They thought the world of Philip. After all, if it hadn't been for his cousin, John might not be with them today.

People who didn't know their family might wonder why Jen or John's parents hadn't given him a kidney. Jen would have if she'd had one to give, but she was one of the small percentage of people who were born with only one kidney. And at the time John so desperately needed one, his father had just had a triple bypass, so he wasn't a candidate. His mother wanted to be the donor, but their doctor had advised against it. It seemed one of her kidneys had problematic function.

When Philip became aware of the problem, he had immediately stepped forward. John hadn't even had to ask.

And this is the way you repay him? You lust after the woman he's fallen for? What kind of jerk does that?

John *had* to forget about Claudia.

He set his jaw. From now on, she was off-limits.

Even in his thoughts.

* * *

On Wednesday John decided he would call an apartment locator and check out what was available. He wanted to move out of Philip's place as soon as possible. Ordinarily, he would enjoy staying with his cousin for a while, but the whole Claudia situation had put a damper on that.

Because no matter what he'd told himself the other day, his spirit might be willing, but his body could very well be weak. No, it would be better for everyone concerned if John were removed from temptation's path. That way he could more easily stick to his resolution.

The woman he talked with at the apartment locator's office was enthusiastic and said she had half a dozen places she could show him that day. Thirty minutes later, he met her at her midtown office. She looked just the way he'd imagined: frizzy bottle-blond hair and unbelievably bright green eyes—obviously the result of colored contact lenses, because no real human had eyes that color. She was small and fairly bristling with energy.

"Hi!" she said, pumping his hand furiously. "Monica Schuller."

Jeez, she had a grip like iron! "John Renzo." He rubbed his hand. Maybe he'd better start working out.

"Are you ready? Let's get going. Do you want to drive? Or do you want me to?" Her questions came rapid-fire.

"I'll drive. Where are we going?"

She flipped open a well-worn notebook. "First place is just blocks away. On Weslayan. Near Bissonnet."

That would be a pretty good location for John. If he lived there, he'd only be about ten minutes from Buffalo Films' headquarters near Westpark and the Loop. "All right. Let's go."

The apartment turned out to be horrible. Old and ugly with a too-small bathroom and inadequate air-conditioning. "No," John said. "I don't think so."

Monica shrugged. "I figured that's what you'd say, but I had to show it to you because of the location. You'll like the next one. It's new."

It was also more money than John wanted to spend. Far more. So he said no to that one, too. If Monica was disappointed, she hid it well.

The third apartment they looked at turned out to be in an excellent location—Greenbriar at Alabama—and it was perfect. John not only liked the layout of the apartment itself, but its placement in the complex was good, too. Far enough away from the pool so he wouldn't have to worry about noisy pool parties, but convenient to the parking area. It was an all-adult complex and he liked that, too. Not that he didn't enjoy kids. He did. Just not in the close confines of apartment living.

The rent was more than he'd hoped to pay but still within his price range. "Do you have anything else in as good a location that costs less?"

Monica shook her head. "The others are farther away and almost as expensive."

"Okay. I'm sold."

An hour later, after John had written a check for the first and last months' rent and signed a lease, Monica said that as soon as his credit check was complete, she'd call him and he could take possession.

He was whistling when he arrived at Philip's townhouse.

"Hey, John, glad you're home," Philip said when John walked in. "I was just going to call you on your cell. You got any plans for Saturday night?"

John shook his head. "No. Why?"

"'Cause I scored four tickets to the Astros game. Think you can get a date?"

John laid his keys, wallet and cell phone on the table in the entryway. He knew what was coming next and he wished he'd been quicker on the draw before saying he had no plans for Saturday.

"I'm going to ask Claudia," Philip went on, oblivious to John's inner turmoil, "and I thought you might like to ask someone and we could double-date."

What could he say now? He'd already said he had no plans. He really had no choice but to agree. "Okay. Sure. Sounds good." *Ah, hell, be honest. No matter what you said about forgetting her, you can't wait to see Claudia again. Under any circumstances.*

"Who're you going to ask? Vicki?"

"Yeah. Probably." Why not? Vicki was fun. And she'd hinted, when they'd met at the party, that she'd like to hear from him again.

Later, when he called her and she said she'd love to go, he wished he could go back and change things. This was a bad idea. A very bad idea.

And yet, he couldn't avoid Claudia forever. If she and Phil *did* get serious about each other and, say, Phil married her, John couldn't avoid seeing her.

He'd have to learn to deal with being around her.

So he might as well start now.

Claudia arrived at school early Thursday morning. For a change, traffic had been light and she'd made record time. She was going through her notes for her first class when Philip poked his head into her classroom. "Got a minute?"

"Sure." She geared herself up to say no if he had come by to ask her out.

Sure enough, that's what he wanted. He said his dad had been given four box seats for the Astros game on Saturday night and had given them to him. "I thought you might enjoy doubling with my cousin and his date."

Claudia swallowed. *His.* He meant John, not Jen. Her heart beat faster at just the thought of seeing John again.

Claudia knew she should say no. It was cruel to

keep dating Philip when their relationship would never go further than friendship.

And yet...*John.*

Taking a deep breath, she said, "Okay. That sounds like fun."

After Philip left, Claudia couldn't deny the frisson of excitement that whispered through her body.

She swallowed.

This was crazy. Philip was going to be her date. Not John. She would just be tormenting herself by going. Not to mention how really rotten it was to continue allowing Philip to think there was any kind of future for them.

You should march yourself down to Philip's office this very minute and tell him you forgot that your mother wants you to come home this weekend, so you can't go to the game with him.

But even as Claudia told herself this, she knew she wasn't going to. The desire to see John again was too strong.

Claudia immediately disliked Vicki Casper, who turned out to be the bubbly, pretty redhead she'd seen John talking to at Jennifer's birthday party. Claudia realized within five minutes of being in her and John's company that the evening was going to be torture.

It wasn't so bad while the four of them—Claudia and Philip, John and Vicki—were at Minute Maid

Park watching the Astros play the Blue Jays. It was noisy and crowded and there was no hand-holding or kissy-face going on between John and Vicki, so Claudia could relax and almost forget John was only one seat away.

But later, in the Cajun seafood restaurant they'd chosen for dinner, it was excruciating for her to watch John and Vicki together, especially because Vicki hung on his every word and acted like he was the best thing since the invention of the cell phone.

"John's started a really interesting project," Philip said after they'd placed their order.

"Oh, tell us about it, John!" Vicki squealed. "What you do is *so* exciting!" She gave him an admiring look. "I never thought I'd know a real, live *filmmaker!*"

Oh, please, Claudia thought. But even she had to admit that John's project did sound fascinating. "Can I ask you something?" she said when he'd finished telling them about it.

His gaze met hers and something inside of her tightened. "Sure," he said.

"Do you ever get bored with your work?"

He smiled, his eyes crinkling up in a way that she liked. "I was bored spitless on my last job. 'Cause even though what I do seems glamorous to people who work in more ordinary professions, it *is* a job, and like any job, it can become routine. Plus some of the projects themselves are boring."

"Oh, I can't *believe* you're ever bored," Vicki exclaimed. "You're certainly not *boring.*"

Had she just scooted her chair closer to John's? Could the girl *be* any more obvious? Claudia hoped the dislike she felt didn't show in her eyes.

"Well, thank you, ma'am," John said.

Vicki giggled.

Claudia hated that giggle. So juvenile.

"You and Jen are both so talented," Vicki said. Now she was making cow eyes at him.

Claudia thought she was going to throw up.

Philip leaned over and asked her quietly, "Is something wrong?"

Claudia quickly shook her head. "No, of course not." *Get a grip,* she told herself. Just then Vicki giggled again and the sound made Claudia grit her teeth. She forced herself not to look across the table but to train her gaze on Philip instead. She smiled. "I'm fine, Philip, really. Just tired. It's been a tough week."

He nodded sympathetically. "We'll make it an early night."

Why did he have to be so nice? *I don't deserve for you to be nice to me,* she thought in a torrent of guilt. *I'm a terrible person.*

Finally the meal was over and the check had been presented and paid, and the four of them were walking out to the parking lot. Although they'd gone to the game in Philip's car, they'd stopped by to pick up

John's car on the way to the restaurant so that John could take Vicki home to Sugar Land on his own.

The two vehicles were parked side by side.

"See you later," Philip said to John. "Good night, Vicki."

"Good night."

John's gaze met Claudia's. "Good night, Claudia. It was nice to see you again."

"You, too." She forced herself to smile at Vicki. "I enjoyed seeing you again, too, Vicki."

Five minutes later, Claudia and Philip were on their way to her condo, and John and Vicki had gone in the other direction.

Considerately, Philip didn't try to make conversation, making Claudia feel even more guilty.

He was almost too nice, she thought. Certainly too nice for her.

Maybe I should be honest with him. Just come right out and tell him he's a great guy, and I like him a lot, but—

But what?

But I'm never going to feel anything more than friendship for you.

Oh, God. How could she say that? She wasn't sure she had it in her to be so blunt. Or maybe she could say she wasn't ready for a serious relationship.

Damn. Why did I go out with him to begin with?

By the time he pulled up in front of her condo, she

knew she couldn't tell him the truth. Not tonight, anyway. Maybe another time when she didn't feel so miserable and could find the right words so that he wouldn't be hurt.

On the other hand, wouldn't it be kinder and easier for everyone if she just kept making excuses when he asked her out? Eventually he'd get the hint.

She hoped.

Chapter Four

"Good night, Vicki. It was fun."

John had just walked her to the door of her second-floor apartment. He leaned down to give her a peck on the cheek before making his getaway.

"Aren't you going to come in?" Vicki giggled, moving closer. "I don't bite." She slid her arms around his waist. "And I'm not against sex on a first date."

John blinked. In all his years of dating, he had never received such a blatant offer. "Well, um, the thing is," he floundered, "I'm, uh, shy." He felt like an idiot, but *jeez*.

"I know the solution to that." So saying, she rubbed against him suggestively. "Just leave everything to me. You won't be shy long."

Whoa.

Grasping her upper arms firmly, he edged her away from him. "Look, I'm flattered, but I, um…I don't like to jump into things." This was true when it came to women, yet in his heart he knew if it were Claudia issuing the invitation, he'd already be inside. Of course, if this were Claudia standing here, she would *never* do or say anything even close. He might not know Claudia well, but he'd bet his life on that.

Vicki shrugged and sighed elaborately. *"Okaaay.* Can't blame a gal for trying." Raising up on her tiptoes, she kissed *his* cheek. "You're a sweet guy, John. Thanks for a fun night. I hope you'll call me again."

As John walked to his car, he thought about how nutty life could be. Vicki was, on all counts, a very desirable woman. She was pretty, she had a knockout figure, she was smart and she was fun. The kind of girl that would cause most red-blooded guys to trample their best friend if they thought they had a chance to score with her.

So what was *his* problem?

He was red-blooded and he liked sex as much as anyone. But Vicki's offer hadn't tempted him in the least. In fact, he could hardly wait to get away from her and her innuendo and her giggle.

Damn. That giggle.

It nearly drove him batty during dinner. A couple of times he'd wondered what Claudia was thinking. He'd caught her giving Vicki funny looks.

Claudia wasn't a giggler. The fact was, Vicki might be smart, but she acted kind of silly. Claudia was anything but silly.

Oh, for crying out loud, quit rationalizing. You aren't interested in Vicki because right now Claudia is the only female in your radar zone.

Yeah, he thought glumly as he drove back to Philip's place. He probably would have liked Vicki just fine if it hadn't been for Claudia. He'd probably be in Vicki's bed right now having hot, sweaty, inventive sex instead of riding home all by his lonesome.

You need to get over this ridiculous obsession with Claudia. She's out of bounds, remember? If you keep this up, you'll never have sex again.

He couldn't help laughing, yet the situation wasn't funny. It was frustrating. The question was, how did he make himself move on when neither his brain nor his body seemed willing to cooperate?

Claudia dreamed about John that night. In her dream, they were lying on a hot, sandy beach. The sun shone brightly in a cloudless sky, causing the surface of the aquamarine water to sparkle with thousands of diamonds of light. A few feet away, the waves broke with a rhythmic, soothing sound. Nearby, palm trees swayed in the balmy breeze, adding their soft swish to the sweet notes of a guitar that was playing softly somewhere in the background.

She was sprawled face down on a blanket, and John, knees on either side of her, was spreading suntan lotion on her back. He'd untied the strings of her bikini top so that he had free access. His strong hands kneaded and stroked, up and down, up and down, from the lowest tip of her spine to her shoulders and neck. A delicious heat bloomed wherever he touched.

Claudia's breathing became ragged as she grew more and more aroused. And when his hands slid down to caress the sides of her breasts, she groaned.

"John…"

He bent down to whisper in her ear, and at the same time slipped his hands underneath her to find her nipples. "Let's go inside." His tongue touched her ear, then he gently bit.

By now Claudia would have agreed to anything, just as long as she'd be doing it with John. He helped her up, then hand in hand, they walked back to their cottage, which was gloriously private and sheltered by a wall of flowering oleander bushes.

Inside, they headed straight for the bedroom. Sunlight striped the wooden floor and fans whirred overhead. In seconds, they'd divested themselves of their bathing suits and were tangled, naked, on the cool sheets. The mosquito netting around the bed made it seem as if they were in a cocoon, totally shut off from the outside world.

Claudia sighed with pleasure, drunk from the sun

and sea and John's caresses. As he trailed kisses down her body, she arched, aching, wanting, needing this and more. His fingers delved, then his tongue.

"Oh!" she cried, opening herself to him.

And then she woke up.

Her heart was pounding.

It took her a moment to realize the wonderful dream had been just that. She and John weren't in Mexico or Hawaii or wherever she'd imagined. She was here alone, and he...he was probably in bed with Vicki.

Claudia wanted to cry. Her body ached with unfulfilled need. Disappointment and frustration and something else, something stronger...anger...warred inside.

Life wasn't fair!

Why *hadn't* John given her the right business card?

Why weren't *they* together tonight, the way Claudia knew they should be?

Oh, John, John...

The tears couldn't be held back any longer. Collapsing onto her pillow, she sobbed out her unhappiness until there were no more tears left.

The pre-production planning meeting was over by one-thirty on Wednesday, which gave John a couple of hours to look over some of the other locations where—in addition to those at the hospital—segments of the Fairchild video would be shot.

But on his way out to the parking lot, John thought about going furniture shopping instead. He was moving into his new apartment over the coming weekend, and right now all he had in the way of furnishings were a bed and a fifty-four-inch television set that would be delivered on Saturday, plus a kitchen table and chairs his parents had donated.

He needed to buy living room furniture—at least a couch and a comfortable chair or maybe a sectional sofa. He could also use a coffee table and a lamp. Once he had the essentials, he could take his time finding the other things he wanted.

Now he wished he hadn't gotten rid of his furniture when he'd moved in with Allison, but what was done was done. Anyway, what the hell. It would be kind of nice to have mostly new stuff.

Jen had recommended a furniture outlet store near downtown where you could get great deals on good brands, so John decided he'd go there first. Maybe he'd get lucky, find everything he wanted in one place and still have time to check out some locations for the video.

He was only blocks from the outlet store when he realized how close he was to Bayou City College…and Claudia. The clock on the dashboard read 1:50, which reminded him of something Claudia had mentioned during dinner Saturday night. They'd been talking about vacation time and John had told Philip and

Claudia they should never complain about their jobs because of all the time they got off.

"Not to mention that you also have a shorter work-day," he'd added, knowing Philip's day ended at four, and Claudia probably had even shorter days.

Both Philip and Claudia had jumped all over him, saying they'd stack the amount of hours they spent on the job against the hours he spent any day of the week. And Claudia had said something to the effect that even though she was through with her last class at two on Mondays and Wednesdays, she still had hours of work ahead of her when she got home.

"Sometimes I'm still working at eight or nine."

"Okay, okay, I stand corrected," John said.

Now, as if his car had a life of its own, John found himself turning toward the college instead of going on to the outlet store.

What the hell are you doing?

But he knew.

He was going to try to "accidentally" bump into Claudia as she left the school. He was going to pretend he'd dropped by to see Philip who, he knew, had a meeting this afternoon, because he'd told John this morning he'd probably be home late.

Have you, from the moment you left the studio, been subconsciously intending to do this instead of shopping?

He swallowed.

It's not too late. Turn around. Go to the furniture store.

But John knew he wasn't going to do that. The need to see Claudia again was too strong.

Maybe she's grown warts. Maybe if I see her again, alone, I won't even like her. That would be good, wouldn't it?

He pushed away the guilt and the knowledge that he was doing something lousy. Something no amount of rationalizing could justify. Something he would not be able to explain to Philip if Philip should ever question him.

Even so, he kept going.

Five minutes later, he pulled into the visitors' parking lot at the college. From his vantage point, he could see the staff lot. In fact, he could see Claudia's Jeep in the second row back. When he saw her walk out, he would call to her, pretend he had come to see Philip and just remembered his cousin was in a meeting.

He looked at his watch. It was two o'clock. If she didn't come out by two-fifteen, he would leave.

As he waited, guilt and excitement competed for dominance.

You should be ashamed of yourself. This is wrong. Claudia is Philip's territory.

He was just about ready to start the truck again when he saw her. She had exited the building and was heading for her Jeep. John opened the door of his car, got out and sprinted across the parking lot to the fence that divided the two areas. "Claudia!"

She stopped, turned around, hesitated, then slowly walked toward him.

"I thought that was you," he said as she drew closer.

"Hi, John. What are *you* doing here?"

Her smile was dazzling. It made him feel light-headed. "I was in the area and stopped by to see Phil, but before I'd even gone inside, I remembered he has a meeting this afternoon." When she didn't say anything, he added, "Anyway, I was just about to leave when I spied you."

For a moment, they stood there awkwardly. Then they both spoke at once.

"What were you—"

"Would you like—"

They both laughed.

"What were you going to say?" he said.

"I just wondered if you were working in the area."

"No, I was heading toward a furniture outlet my sister told me about. It's only a few blocks from here."

"I think I know the one you mean. Diamond's?"

"Yeah, that's the one."

"You're moving into your apartment this weekend?"

"Yeah. And I need living room stuff. Hey, you wouldn't by any chance have an hour to spare, would you? I could sure use a female perspective on what to buy."

She gave him a funny look. "Oh, come on, a creative guy like you? I'll bet you have great taste."

"Just because a person is creative in one field doesn't mean he's got any ability in another." He was getting good at embellishing the truth.

She smiled. "Okay. Sure. I'd enjoy going with you. I like that place. They've got great stuff."

"Great." He felt as if he'd just won the lottery, but he was trying to be cool and not show it. "We can ride in my truck, then I'll bring you back here. If that's okay?"

"Sure. Let me put this stuff in my Jeep first."

"Okay. I'll get the car and come pick you up."

Five minutes later they were on their way. John was acutely conscious of her sitting next to him. He kept sneaking glances at her profile. God, she was beautiful. No matter what she wore, she looked perfect to him. Today she had on fitted black pants with a scoop-necked white T-shirt underneath a wine-colored jacket. The T-shirt hugged her body, clearly delineating small, perfect-looking breasts. He swallowed. He wanted her so badly it was all he could do to keep from touching her.

She turned and caught him looking at her. She didn't say anything, but John was afraid she knew exactly what he was thinking.

Thank God they had now reached the outlet store. John forced his attention back to his driving.

By the time they'd parked and walked into the store, he had himself under better control. Still, he was all too aware of her beside him, of the faint flowery scent of her perfume, of her confident, lanky stride, and especially of the way all eyes followed her as they walked toward the living room section. Yeah, she was something special all right, and everyone knew it.

"What style of furniture do you like?" she asked when they'd reached the display of couches. "No, wait. Let me guess. Contemporary and sleek, right?"

John smiled. "I'm flattered you think I'm that kind of guy."

"You mean you aren't?"

"Maybe half. I like stuff that has clean lines, but I'm not into the real minimal look." He pointed to a sectional sofa that was upholstered in a warm brown suede. "That's the kind of thing I like. Suede and leather and comfortable looking with real deep cushions."

"Colors?"

John shrugged. "I'm open. The apartment walls are all white, so I can do anything."

"But what colors do you *like?*"

"Blues and grays and browns mostly."

She grinned. "Really? That's pretty close to my color scheme."

He grinned, too. He couldn't help it. He wanted to say he was pretty sure he'd like anything she liked, but he knew it was dangerous to get into that territory so he stayed silent.

For the next thirty minutes they looked at just about every sofa in the place, and there were a lot of them. Some they just glanced at, then made faces at each other. It was amazing how similar their tastes were. Almost every time she liked something, he did, too.

After narrowing his choices down to three, he tested sitting on them and then lying down on them and made her do the same.

"Why does it matter if I do?" she said, laughing.

"Because you're a girl. I want to be sure whatever I pick is as comfortable for a girl as it is for me."

John's favorite ended up being a sectional sofa upholstered in a golden-brown fabric that simulated suede. "What do you think?"

"I think it's a great choice."

"You're not just saying that?"

"What's the matter? Don't you trust your own taste?" she teased.

"It's not that. I just want to be sure *you* like it."

Suddenly the undercurrents between them leaped into life. Looking into her eyes, John was sure she felt them as strongly as he did. At that moment, all he wanted to do was pull her into his arms and say, "I'm crazy about you. You know that, don't you?"

What he did instead was force his gaze away. Taking a deep breath, he said, "Now I need a couple of tables to go with it."

By the time they'd picked out a coffee table and matching end table in a dark, distressed wood they'd also picked up a salesman who wanted to sell John an entertainment center to house his new TV set.

But John stayed firm. He wasn't sure he wanted an entertainment center. He might rather spend his money on stuff for the bedroom.

John put the furniture on his Visa card, paid the fee to have it delivered—one of the reasons the furniture cost less was the fact there wasn't free delivery—and then he and Claudia headed out.

"How about letting me buy you a cup of coffee and a doughnut or something?" John said. "Pay you back for helping me out."

"That sounds good."

Those eyes of hers did things to him. They were great eyes. Big and blue. And when she talked, she looked straight at him.

Face it. You like everything about her.

"Do you have a favorite place around here for coffee?" he asked when they were underway.

"Actually, I do. It's a little coffee shop a block away from the school."

After giving him directions, she said, "I think you're going to be really happy with what you bought."

"Yeah, me too."

"You'll have to have a housewarming party."

"That's a good idea. I like any excuse for a party." He smiled at her. "Will you come?"

"I wouldn't miss it. Oh, there's the coffee shop."

Once they were settled at their table and had placed their orders—plain black coffee and a blueberry muffin for him, coffee with cream and a cranberry muffin for her—John said, "You mentioned that this is your first year of teaching?"

"Yes."

"What did you do before that?"

"Nothing very interesting. I worked in the marketing department of a fairly large company."

"Selling?"

"No. More like marketing strategies. That kind of thing."

"What kind of company was it?"

She hesitated just long enough to make John wonder why. Then she shrugged. "Look, I was bored working there, and it's even more boring to talk about it. Let's talk about something else, okay?"

John wondered if there was something she was reluctant to divulge. He couldn't imagine what it might be. But her reaction to his question, especially that slight hesitation, made him curious. "All right. How do you like living in Houston so far?"

Now she smiled. "Oh, I love it. There's so much to

do here. And the shopping! It's wonderful, even better than Dallas, I think."

"Yeah, my mother and sister think the shopping is great, too. It can be hard on your credit cards, though."

"I never charge more than I can pay off the next month," she said.

She was definitely a girl after his own heart, for John did not believe in debt. He'd gone that route once, with unhappy consequences, but never again. He'd learned his lesson. Now, if he didn't have the money, he didn't buy it.

Just then the woman who Claudia said was the owner signaled that their order was ready and John excused himself to go and pick it up. When he returned to the table, they resumed their conversation.

"How did *you* feel about leaving Austin and moving here?" she asked.

"I was ready for a change, both professionally and personally."

She nodded. "I hope you don't mind, but Philip mentioned you broke up with your girlfriend recently." She stirred sweetener into her coffee and took a sip.

Now why had Philip had to mention that? John wondered. "No, I don't mind. It's not a secret."

"Well, I'm sorry."

"Nothing to be sorry about. Tell you the truth, I'm relieved."

"That's good, then." She broke off a piece of her muffin and ate it.

"I *have* had my heart broken a time or two, though."

"You have?"

"Hasn't everyone?" He grinned. "The first time was in the fifth grade when I had this enormous crush on Mary Sue Lassiter, but she liked Mark Connelly instead."

Claudia laughed.

John loved her laugh. It made her eyes crinkle up at the corners. "And then in high school I was sick in love with Debbie Marsh, who was this really cute cheerleader. I don't know what I was thinking. Hell, she thought I was a weirdo. She actually told me that. Her true love was the quarterback of the football team. I'm not exactly the football type." He shrugged. "Even then, I was into film. Of course, *then* I imagined I'd be a big shot Hollywood director." He buttered his muffin and took a big bite.

"I can't imagine you as anything but popular," Claudia said.

"I had some good friends, but I didn't do the cool things that make you popular in high school. I got good grades but I didn't fit in with the brains. I didn't play sports so the jocks wanted nothing to do with me. I wasn't into drugs, so the druggies ignored me." He shrugged. "Like I said, I had good friends. Being popular wasn't high on my agenda."

"What about Philip? Was he popular?"

"He was kind of shy when he was younger. We didn't go to the same high school, you know."

"Oh, I didn't know that. I just assumed, from what he's told me that you two have been best friends all of your lives."

"Our families are close, but he's two years younger than me…and going to different schools and all…we didn't really start hanging out together until he graduated from college." He buttered another section of muffin. "That's enough talk about me. Now I want to hear about you. I'll bet you were the most sought-after, popular girl in high school." He finished off his muffin and brushed the crumbs off his lap.

Claudia thought about the all-girl school her grandmother had insisted she and her sisters attend because of course the local high school wasn't good enough for a Hathaway. "I went to an all-girl school. I had friends, but I wouldn't say I was popular."

"You went to an all-girl school? A church school or something?"

"Yes, a Catholic high school in San Antonio. I boarded."

"So you're Catholic? So am I."

"No," Claudia said, almost regretting it now that she knew he was. "But my grandmother, who's pretty strict, talked my mother into sending me and my sisters there. Guess she thought it was safer than the public schools." Kathleen Hathaway had wanted to send her daughters to an exclusive finishing school in Charleston, but had finally given in to Claudia's grandmother's choice.

"So what was it like going to an all-girl school?"

"It was okay. I liked it."

"What about guys? Did you date in high school?"

"Occasionally. There was this one boy, the brother of one of my classmates. He was nice. We went out a few times when I was a senior."

"So you didn't get your heart broken in high school like I did, huh?"

Claudia ate a bite of her muffin. "I didn't say that." She liked when he smiled at her like that, as if she amused him in a really nice way.

"I'm waiting," he said. "I bared my soul, now you've gotta bare yours."

Claudia smiled. "I had this *huge* crush on my Spanish teacher. Oh, God, he was gorgeous. He was in his late twenties and had these soulful dark eyes and dark hair. I was mad for him." Come to think of it, John had that same look about him. "And crushed when I found out he was engaged. I cried for days."

"What about college? Any serious attachments?"

"Nope. I almost got pinned once, but I changed my mind. Decided he drank too much. I'd had enough of that in my family."

John didn't press for details, and for that, Claudia

was grateful. It saddened her that her father had wasted so much of his life in an alcoholic haze. Was *still* wasting it. She knew her mother would have left him long ago if it weren't for the family's position and money.

By now they'd finished their food. Claudia looked at her watch. It was nearly four-thirty. Reluctantly, she said, "It's getting late, and I have a test to grade and reading to do."

"Say no more." He dug in his pocket and put a couple of crumpled dollar bills on the table.

"You don't have to leave a tip."

"I know. I want to."

He was so nice. Why couldn't he have two heads and be conceited or something?

It only took a couple of minutes for him to drive her back to the school. When they got there, he pulled into the faculty lot and stopped his truck behind her Jeep. Then he got out and walked around to open her door for her.

He helped her down, and just that brief touch of his hand caused butterflies in Claudia's stomach. Oh, she liked this man. She liked him way too much. And there wasn't a darned thing she could do about it. Unless she asked *him* out, since it didn't look as if he would ask her. Did she dare? Oh, she wanted to. But something held her back. He might say no. And then she would have ruined any chance she had. Pushing these dangerous thoughts out of her mind, she smiled and said, "Thanks for the coffee and muffin. It hit the spot."

"I should be thanking *you*. You were a big help at Diamond's. Thanks for coming with me."

And then there really wasn't anything more to say except goodbye.

Chapter Five

Claudia couldn't stop thinking about the coffee date—as she'd begun to call it in her mind.

She'd had so much fun.

She'd loved picking out furniture with John. She'd spent the whole time fantasizing, pretending they were a couple furnishing an apartment or condo they were going to share.

And their conversation at the coffee shop had been a revelation. She loved the way that, instead of pumping himself up like so many of her past dates had, he told less than flattering stories about himself and laughed at his own foibles. Claudia could never be with a man who took himself too seriously.

She considered a sense of humor essential. She had a feeling, though, that John had probably exaggerated his lack of popularity in high school. She didn't care what he'd said, she couldn't imagine any girl *not* liking him. But it was sweet of him to pretend otherwise.

After thinking about him so much, it had been a shock to run into him in the parking lot of the school. Almost as if it had been fated. And yet…she couldn't help wondering if John had told her the truth.

Had he really been at the college to see Philip and had just happened to see her there instead? She wasn't sure why she was questioning his explanation, only that something in the way he'd acted had planted a kernel of suspicion that refused to go away.

What if he'd come to the college purposely to see her? The thought filled her with such happiness, she wanted to laugh out loud.

She sighed.

What real difference would it make if he had? Even if he'd wanted to be with her the way she'd dreamed about being with him, what could they possibly do about it? The very fact that John *was* so decent and didn't think the world revolved around him and his desires told her he'd never purposely hurt Philip. All she could do was wait. Eventually Philip would have to give up, and then maybe she and John would have a chance.

If only being with John that afternoon had revealed

something distasteful about him, something that would have turned Claudia off the way she'd been turned off before by so many other guys she'd first thought nice.

But no.

Far from dimming the attraction, the time she'd spent with John had only made her like him more. This was *such* a frustrating situation. She was positive John felt the connection between them. It was there, in his voice and in his eyes. There was an invisible current they were both aware of, yet couldn't acknowledge openly, because in addition to that current was the ever-present specter of Philip.

This whole thing was so not fair, Claudia thought, mentally fuming in impotent frustration. If only there were something she could do to change things now, but there wasn't.

Not knowing what else to do, but realizing she had to do *something*, she called her sister Lorna. Of all the women Claudia knew—and this was definitely a subject to talk over with another woman— her sister Lorna was the most sensible and clear-headed when it came to sizing up a problem and finding a solution.

"So let me see if I have this straight," Lorna said. "You've met this guy and you really like him and you think he really likes you, but he'll never ask you out because his cousin saw you first."

"Well, actually, John saw me first but—"

"I know, but Philip asked you out first and he keeps asking you out."

"Yes," Claudia said glumly.

"You haven't encouraged him, though."

"No…not really."

"What does that mean?"

"Well, after our first date I decided I wasn't going to go out with him again since it was obvious to me the relationship was never going to go anywhere. But then when he asked me out again, it was to double-date with John, and I…" Claudia didn't like confessing this part. "The truth is, I couldn't resist the opportunity to see John again, so I said yes."

"Claudia."

Claudia winced at Lorna's disappointed tone. "I know. I shouldn't have gone."

"No, you shouldn't have. If you knew you weren't interested in Philip, it wasn't fair to him to go. I mean, what did *that* say?"

"I know," Claudia said again. Because she *did* know. It had, in fact, been rotten of her to accept that last date. It had been misleading and selfish. Philip was also a very nice man, too nice to give him false encouragement. "I won't do it again."

"Good."

"Okay, so what's your advice? Aside from not accepting any more dates with Philip."

"I'd just give the whole situation time. Who knows?

From what you've said, Philip isn't stupid. Once he realizes things aren't going to work out with you, maybe he'll find someone else. Then the field with John will be clear."

"But what if—" Claudia broke off.

"What if what?"

"What if John gets tired of waiting around? What if *he* finds someone else?" Claudia couldn't help thinking about Vicki, the giggler, who also happened to be extremely sexy, even though Claudia hated admitting it.

"You know the answer to that."

"No, I don't," Claudia said stubbornly.

"Yes, you do. If John finds someone else, then he's not the man for you."

Claudia muttered a not-nice word.

"I know," her sister said gently. "Sometimes the truth is hard to face."

"It's just that I have never met anyone I liked as much. I…" Claudia swallowed. "I think I could love him." Then, since she was baring her soul, she decided to bare it even further. "No, I *know* I could love him. I, oh, Lorna, maybe I…already love him."

"Hon, I wish I had some magic answer for you, but I don't. From what you've told me about both men, I think, at this stage, if you were to tell Philip and John the truth about your feelings, you might lose both of them."

"But I don't *want* Philip," Claudia cried. "I'd *like* to lose *him!*"

"You know that's not what I meant."

"Oh, I know, I'm just so *frustrated.*"

"That much is obvious," Lorna said dryly. "Even if you *hadn't* told me twice, I would have guessed."

"I'm sorry. I shouldn't have called you."

"Are you going to persist in twisting everything I say? I'm glad you called me. What are sisters for if they can't vent their frustrations to each other? Now stop feeling sorry for yourself and go out and do something nice for somebody. It'll take your mind off your troubles. Believe me, I know."

Immediately, Claudia felt bad. Lorna *did* know, better than most. She'd caught her husband in bed with his twenty-year-old assistant. And she'd never felt sorry for *herself.* "Okay. Point taken."

"Good."

"And Lorna? Thanks."

"No thanks necessary. Love you, kid."

"Love you, too."

John decided he'd better tell Philip about "running into" Claudia in case she happened to mention something about the furniture shopping or having coffee together. Because even though he'd ignored his conscience and done something he shouldn't have, John hated going behind Philip's back, and he didn't want to hurt him anymore than he might have already.

So when Philip got home—after eight because he'd gone to dinner when his meeting was over—John casually said, "Hey, guess what? I forgot you had that meeting today and stopped by the school to see you."

"Really? Sarah didn't say anything."

"I didn't go inside. I was just about to when I remembered you were tied up."

Philip picked up the mail sitting on a table by the door. "Why'd you come? Did you need something?"

John shrugged. "No. I was on my way to Diamond's to pick out some furniture and thought since I was in the area, I'd stop in, say hello to you and Sarah."

"Oh, well, sorry about that. Come by another time. Sarah will enjoy seeing you. She asks about you all the time." Philip grinned. "I think she has a thing for you."

John doubted that. From what he'd seen of Sarah, she had a thing for Philip. He almost said so, then thought better of it. He didn't want to cause Philip to feel awkward around her, and knowing his cousin, he probably would.

"Anyway," he said instead, "I ran into Claudia."

Philip stopped leafing through the mail and looked up. "Oh?"

"Yeah, it was a lucky thing for me, 'cause I managed to talk her into giving me some help."

Philip set the mail down. "With what?"

John shrugged. "I wanted a woman's opinion on furniture, so I talked her into going to Diamond's with me."

Philip frowned and John geared himself up for what was coming, like "Why didn't you have Jen or your mother go with you?"

But the frown disappeared and all his cousin said was "That was nice of her."

"Yeah, it was, and she gave me some good suggestions. Afterwards, she said I should have a housewarming party once I get moved."

Philip picked up the mail again and began to open one of the envelopes.

"Anyway," John continued doggedly, "I was grateful for her help, so I bought her coffee afterward."

Philip looked up again. Was that a glimmer of suspicion in his eyes? But all he said was, "So what do you think of her?"

John relaxed. Phil wasn't suspicious. It was John's own guilty conscience that had made him think he might be. "I think you have good taste. She's nice. I like her."

Philip grinned. "Did she mention me?" It was asked casually, but John knew it was not a casual question.

"Yeah, she did."

"What did she say?"

"Just something about you telling her about Allison and me breaking up, that was all."

"Oh."

"So how was the meeting? Get anything productive done?" John really wanted to change the subject, for the longer they talked about Claudia and today, the worse he felt.

"Yeah, we finally agreed on a budget. No one got everything they wanted, but we managed to give every department something. I don't know, though. Seems to me we're going to have to raise tuition next year. The bottom line is, we can't cut another thing without cutting quality."

Grateful that he'd distracted his cousin, John listened as Philip warmed up to his subject, even though he'd lost interest. But he owed Philip big-time for the underhanded thing he'd done today, and the fact Philip didn't realize it didn't make the owing any less true.

For the remainder of the evening Claudia thought about Lorna's advice. She was still thinking about it the next day when, after her morning class, Philip came by her classroom.

"Want to grab some pizza or something for lunch?" he said.

She was prepared. "Thanks, Philip, but I brought my lunch today. I'm going to eat at my desk and go over my notes for my next class."

"Oh, okay." The eager light in his eyes faded.

Claudia fought against feeling sorry for him and guilty for disappointing him.

Dammit! It's not your fault he's latched on to you, and it's not your responsibility to make him happy, either.

Instead of leaving, as she'd thought he would, he advanced farther into the room and sat on the edge of her desk. "I hear you helped my cousin buy some furniture yesterday."

Taken off guard, Claudia stammered a little before getting herself under better control. "I, um, yes, we, um, kind of ran into each other in the parking lot."

"Yeah, that's what he said."

"So, anyway, I, um, went with him."

Oh, for heaven's sake, what was *wrong* with her? Even a five-year-old would sense she felt guilty. And yet, why should she? She hadn't done anything wrong. It wasn't *her* fault she couldn't feel for Philip what she felt for John.

"That was nice of you. To help him out."

Claudia shrugged. "No big deal." She wished he'd go, and to give him the hint, she picked up the notes she intended to read.

"John's a great guy, isn't he?"

"Yes, he is. I like both your cousins."

"He said he got some nice stuff."

"Yes, it's very nice." She looked at the notes. *Was he* ever *going to go?*

He finally said, "Well, I guess you're anxious to get to those notes."

"Yes, I am. There's nothing worse than feeling unprepared."

"I'll leave you to it, then. See you later."

After he'd gone, she shut the door to her office and leaned against it. Damn. She wasn't cut out to be a liar.

Telling herself she hadn't caused this awkward situation, she went back to her desk, took out the sandwich and Braeburn apple she'd brought to eat and forced herself to forget about Philip and John and everything else and concentrate on preparing for her next class.

She didn't see Philip again the rest of the day, and Claudia was grateful for the reprieve.

It was almost six before she got home. She'd had to do some errands on the way, including grocery shopping, and she was tired and—if she were honest—still feeling the tension of the episode with Philip.

But as soon as she walked into her cool, tranquil condo, she felt herself begin to relax.

This was the first time she'd really had a place of her own. Through college she'd roomed with Sally—which was fun—but not the same. And then after graduating and going to work in the family business, she'd lived at home. It had seemed silly not to since the Hathaway estate was so big and she had her own private suite. Then again, though, it hadn't been like having her own place.

She loved her condo. The walls were all painted in soft grays and blues and every stick of furniture was new and chosen by Claudia, reflecting her taste and not her mother's.

She loved the way the sunlight streamed into the kitchen in the mornings and the rain sounded when it fell on the roof. She loved the fireplace and couldn't wait until the weather was cold enough to have a fire.

But most of all, she loved the feeling of safety that enveloped her when she closed the door and shut out the rest of the world.

She had just finished bringing in her groceries and had piled everything onto the kitchen table when the phone rang. Checking caller ID, Claudia saw that the caller was Jennifer Renzo.

Smiling, she punched the On button. "Hello?"

"Hello, Claudia?"

"Yes. Hi, Jennifer."

"Hi. Did I get you in the middle of something?"

"No, not at all. I just got home."

"I've been meaning to call you ever since the party."

"And I've been meaning to call *you*."

"I'm really glad Philip brought you that night."

"Me, too." If she hadn't gone to the party, no telling how long it would have been before she'd met John and found out who he *really* was.

"This might seem strange, but the minute I met you I knew we could be good friends."

"I felt the same way!"

"Did you?"

Claudia could almost hear the smile in the other woman's voice. "Yes, exactly the same."

"Since we feel the same way, why don't we get together for lunch on Saturday."

"I'd love to."

"Great. What area do you live in?"

When Claudia told her, Jennifer said, "You're not that far from me."

"No, I'm not."

"Why don't we plan to eat somewhere around the Galleria, then?" She named several restaurants she thought Claudia might like and they settled on a Thai place Jennifer said was terrific.

"So I'll see you at one on Saturday?"

"It's a date."

When Claudia hung up, she was still smiling.

For the rest of the week, Claudia looked forward to the luncheon. It would be great to see Jennifer again. The only downside to the budding friendship was Jennifer's connection to John. And yet…wasn't that part of her appeal, too?

Be honest. You like the fact she's John's sister because even if you can't see him, you can at least know what's going on in his life.

Saturday morning, she whizzed through her laundry and cleaning chores, then headed for the shower. Forty-five minutes later, she was almost ready to go. The weather had finally cooled down from record highs to a temperate sixty-five degrees, so Claudia wore jeans paired with a pale blue sweater. Black clogs, silver hoop earrings and six silver bracelets completed her outfit.

She arrived at the Thai restaurant five minutes early and she hadn't even gotten out of her Jeep when Jennifer, driving a dark-green SUV, pulled in beside her.

They grinned at one another.

"You're as anal as I am about being on time, am I right?" Jennifer said after they'd hugged hello. She, too, wore jeans, but hers were black. With them she had on a formfitting white blouse with black buttons. Her dark hair was swept back and held in place by a white scrunchie.

"Guilty," Claudia said.

"My reason is I grew up in an Italian Catholic household. What's yours?" Jennifer said.

"A grandmother who thought books on etiquette were proper bedtime reading." Claudia still remembered how her grandmother had drilled into her and her siblings the importance of good manners. "My grandmother always said that people who are late think no one else's time is as important as theirs."

Jennifer grinned. "That's what *my* grandmother always said."

"There's probably a how-to book for grandmothers."

"You think?"

Claudia laughed. "Actually, my grandmother probably didn't need a how-to. She was born smart. And intimidating."

By now they were inside and following the hostess to their booth. Once seated, they took a few minutes to order a pot of tea to share and to study the menu.

When they'd decided what they wanted, they began to talk again.

"I love your sweater," Jennifer said. "Is it silk?"

"Thanks. And yes, it is."

"Well, it's beautiful. The color matches your eyes exactly."

"Actually, I love *your* blouse. I've been looking for something like that for a while."

"Dillard's Memorial City," Jennifer said. At Claudia's blank look, she said, "Haven't you been to Memorial City yet?"

Claudia shook her head. "I haven't gone shopping anywhere but the Galleria."

"Well, you *must* check out Memorial City. If you want to, we can go after lunch. Do you have time?"

"I have nothing else planned for today." Guiltily, she remembered that when he'd suggested going out tonight, she'd told Philip she was probably going to go home for the weekend. "I had thought about going home," she added. "But I didn't want to break our lunch date so decided to just wait until next weekend."

"Where *is* home?"

But just then their waitress came to take their order, and by the time they'd placed it, Jennifer had forgotten she'd asked the question. Claudia didn't remind her. Although she fully intended to tell Jennifer about her family one day, she didn't want to just yet.

While they waited for their hot-and-sour soup, they talked about Jennifer's job. She told Claudia she was thinking about making a change.

"I'm tired of the long hours, and I'm tired of making such a pittance. The thing is, I work like a dog. In fact, I do the work of two people. I'm sick of it."

"But what would you do? Do you have another job lined up?"

"Not yet, but I'm working on it."

"Have you told them how you feel? Your boss, I mean?"

"She knows. She just doesn't care."

"But how do you *know* that?" Claudia asked.

"Trust me. She doesn't care."

They stopped talking because their soup came, but as soon as the waitress was gone, they resumed their discussion of Jennifer's job.

"Well," Claudia said when Jennifer related an incident involving her boss, "I think you should level with her. From what you've said, it sounds to me like she just takes you for granted. I have a feeling if you told her you were thinking of going elsewhere, she'd change her tune. Some people just need to be hit over the head, you know?"

Jennifer shrugged. "I don't know. After you and I talked at the party, I decided it might be time for a complete change. I'm not sure I even *want* to stay with the station. The way I feel is, I don't want to have to threaten them to get what I deserve. You know?"

Claudia nodded, although she had never been in the same kind of situation since her only work experience before teaching had been in her family's company. Still, she could understand how Jennifer felt.

"Let's talk about something else," Jennifer said. "Tell me about your family."

"Well, I have two older sisters and an older brother."

"Where do they live?"

"My oldest sister lives in Austin and the other two live in the little town where I grew up. It's between Austin and San Antonio." Claudia hoped Jennifer wouldn't ask her again about the name of the town.

"That's a nice part of the state."

"Yes, it is."

"I'll bet your family hated for you to move away. I know I hated it when John left to go to Austin." She smiled. "I'm so glad he's back. I really missed him."

"You two are close."

"Well, he's my only sibling. But yes, our whole

family is close, and that includes Philip and his parents."

Jennifer stopped talking while their waitress cleared their soup bowls and served their lunch. But once the waitress left, she said, "You know, all the years we were growing up, the seven of us almost always had Sunday dinner together."

"That's really wonderful."

"It was wonderful."

"What about now? Do you still get together every Sunday?"

"Not as much. We all have our own lives now. You know how it is. Everyone's busy."

Claudia took a bite of her Thai curry chicken. Then, offhandedly, she said, "Philip and John are especially close, aren't they?"

"Yes. They always have been, but since Philip gave John a kidney, they've been even closer."

Claudia nearly choked on her food. "Philip gave John a *kidney?*"

"Oh, I thought you knew. Yes, three years ago. See, John had nephritis when he was ten, and the disease left his kidneys damaged. The doctors said then it was only a matter of time before he'd probably need a new one. I would have given John a kidney, but I only have one."

Claudia was still trying to absorb this stunning revelation.

"Philip never hesitated," Jennifer went on. "No one even had to ask him. He volunteered." She forked some of her pad thai. "He's a wonderful guy."

"No wonder John thinks so highly of him."

"We all do."

Was it Claudia's imagination or was Jennifer trying to get her to say something about how *she* felt about Philip? For just an instant, Claudia was tempted to tell Jennifer the truth. Maybe even enlist her help.

But the urge didn't last long. Claudia knew she couldn't do that. It wouldn't be fair to Jennifer to ask her to choose between her brother and her cousin, and that was exactly what Claudia *would* be doing.

No, Claudia thought in resignation, *this is my problem, no one else's. And I'm the one who has to figure out the solution.*

But now that she knew about the kidney, she was afraid there *was* no solution.

At least, not the one she wanted!

Chapter Six

After four and a half hours of tramping through what seemed like most of the shops at Memorial City Mall, Claudia and Jennifer were both beat, but happy.

"I *love* my new blouse," Claudia said. She'd gotten one identical to Jennifer's. "You're sure you don't mind that I'm copying you?"

"Would I have brought you out here if I did?" Jennifer countered.

Claudia grinned. "Guess not."

"Just as long as you don't wear it when I'm wearing mine."

"What? You don't want to be twins?" Claudia teased.

Jennifer rolled her eyes. "Like anyone would ever mistake us for twins. I *wish*." She eyed Claudia. "You know, I'd kill to have long legs like yours. Oh, and did I mention that blondes have more fun?"

"Oh, come on," Claudia said, embarrassed. "I love the way you look. You remind me of Neve Campbell."

"I *do?*"

"Except you're prettier."

"Oh, now I *know* you're just trying to make me feel good." She smiled. "But I'm easy that way. You've succeeded!"

"I also love my new bracelets!" Claudia held out her wrist to admire the Swarovski brushed silver bangles with the imbedded crystals. "You did notice I'm a bracelet slut?"

Jennifer grinned. "Just because you wear a dozen at a time? But, no, I hadn't noticed."

Claudia decided she and Jennifer had been friends in another life. How else to explain their perfect understanding of each other?

When they reached Jennifer's car—they'd left Claudia's Jeep parked at the restaurant—Jennifer said, "I can't believe it, but I'm actually starting to think about food again."

"Me, too. Sometimes I think I have a tapeworm."

Jennifer laughed. "And I never met a carb I didn't like."

"You sound like my friend Sally. You'd like her. I

hope she comes down for the weekend soon so you two can meet each other."

"Where does she live?"

"In Austin. She was the one I was visiting when I met your brother."

"Oh, really? You met John in Austin? Before you moved here?"

"Yes, didn't you know?"

"Uh-uh."

"Oh. I thought he might have told you. Anyway, back to Sally...she loves to eat, too." Claudia tossed her packages onto the back seat of Jennifer's car.

Jennifer laughed. "Then I *know* I'd like her."

"So speaking of eating, do you want to stop and get a salad or something on the way back?"

Jennifer finished loading her parcels into the car. "I've got a better idea. Why don't we stop and pick up your car and then you follow me to my place? I've got some of this great Australian Shiraz, and in the fridge there's a container of my mom's spaghetti sauce and meatballs. We can listen to music, drink wine, and when we get good and hungry I'll put some pasta on. I think I've even got enough lettuce for salad. What do you say?"

"I say that sounds terrific."

An hour later, the two women stood in Jennifer's cheerful red-and-white kitchen. They chatted and sipped at their wine while listening to the newest Coldplay CD. While the spaghetti sauce and meatballs simmered on the stove, Jennifer began to add pasta to a pot of boiling water.

"So I told him I'd kick his you-know-what if he put his hands anywhere near me again—" Jennifer broke off as the phone rang. "Could you get that, Claudia?"

"Sure." Claudia reached for the phone, which was on the counter behind her. Punching the On button, she said, "Hello?"

"Uh…I think I have the wrong number," said a male voice that sounded suspiciously like John's.

Claudia's heart skipped a beat. "If you're calling Jennifer, you have the right number."

There was a moment of silence. Then, "Claudia? Is that you?"

"Yes. Hi, John. Did you want to speak to your sister? She's standing right here." To Jennifer, she said, "I'll watch the pasta." Then she handed her the phone. Claudia knew she'd been abrupt, but she needed to put on her game face before talking to John in front of his sister. She stirred the pasta.

"Hi, John," Jennifer said. "What's up?" She listened awhile. "Thanks, but we're actually fixing dinner as we speak. But hey, no reason for you to eat alone. Why don't you just come here and have dinner with us? There's plenty."

Oh, no, Claudia thought.

But even as she told herself this was not a good development, excited butterflies danced in her stomach.

"We're having spaghetti and meatballs," Jennifer said. "With Mom's sauce." She listened again. "No, I've got plenty of wine. Tell you what, though. Why don't you stop and pick up some good bread somewhere? I know how you like bread. Yeah. Okay. Great. See you in a bit."

Disconnecting, she placed the phone back on its base. "You don't mind, do you? That John's coming to eat with us."

"No, of course not. Why would I mind?"

"Oh, you know, no more girl talk."

"That's okay. We'll have other times, won't we?"

Jennifer smiled. "I'm counting on it." She walked over to the stove. "That pasta should be just about done. Why don't you taste a piece and see what you think?"

"You do it," Claudia said. "I'm the world's worst cook."

"Claudia, it's not rocket science to taste the pasta for doneness."

"Even so, I'd probably manage to screw it up." One of Claudia's resolutions was to learn to cook now that she had a kitchen of her own.

Jennifer shook her head and lifted a piece of pasta out of the pot. "It's perfect." She shut off the gas.

"How'd you learn to cook?" Claudia asked.

"You don't grow up in an Italian household without learning. My mother insisted on teaching both John and me as soon as we were old enough to read a cookbook."

"Really? John cooks, too?"

"Yup. In fact, I think he's a better cook than I am." Jennifer made a face. "Actually, he's better at just about everything than I am. He's also my mother's favorite, even though she'd never admit it."

"Does that bother you?"

Jennifer shook her head. "Not really. I know she loves me. Besides, I'm my dad's favorite."

Claudia laughed, but underneath the laugh was a twinge of sadness because she had never felt the closeness with her parents that Jennifer and John obviously felt with theirs.

Claudia loved her parents, but she didn't like them very much. Kathleen was too cold, not the kind to dispense hugs and kisses, and Claudia's father was disconnected from his family because of his love affair with the bottle. The warmth and love Claudia got growing up had come from her sisters and brother, and from her Grandmother Hathaway, although hers had been tempered with a tough-minded discipline.

"So your mother never taught you to cook?" Jennifer asked.

"No." Feeling she had to elaborate yet not wanting to confess that she'd grown up in a household with a housekeeper, cook and gardener, she added, "She's the kind who doesn't like a mess." This was true. Kathleen Hathaway expected order and cleanliness at all times.

They continued to talk while Jennifer drained the pasta and put it back into the pot. She poured in a bit of olive oil.

Claudia moved closer to watch. "Why are you doing that?"

"So it won't stick together." Jennifer stirred the oil in.

"But why not just put the sauce over it?"

Their conversation had taken Claudia's mind off John's imminent arrival, but her reprieve was short-lived because the doorbell rang before Jennifer could reply.

"That's John," she said. "Want to let him in?"

Claudia's treacherous heart betrayed her again as she walked out to the front door. She took a deep breath before opening it.

"Hi, John." She was proud of how normal and casual she sounded, considering how he affected her.

"Hi, Claudia."

Their gazes held for a moment and Claudia wondered what he was thinking. Did he, like her, wonder why fate continued to throw them together?

She stepped back to let him in. "Jennifer's in the kitchen." As she led the way, she was acutely conscious of him behind her.

"Hey, bro," Jennifer said when they entered the kitchen.

John put down the loaf of French bread he was carrying and gave his sister a hug. Watching them, Claudia wished she had a right to a hug, too. A hug *and* a kiss. She looked away because she was afraid the longing she felt would show in her eyes.

"So why are you at loose ends tonight?" Jennifer asked. "I thought maybe you'd be out with Vicki." She winked at Claudia. "Or some other hot date."

John made a face. "Some hot date. Phil and I were going to catch a movie or something, but Dan Greavy called him with an extra ticket for the Rockets game. I guess Lily was sick and couldn't go. Phil wasn't going to say yes, but I told him to go. I sure wouldn't pass up the chance to see the Rockets play unless I really *did* have a hot date."

So saying, he glanced at Claudia. She noticed he hadn't addressed Jennifer's comment about Vicki and wondered why.

Almost as if he'd known what she was thinking, he added, "And I'm not going to ask Vicki out again."

"Why not? I thought you two were hitting it off at the party."

John shrugged. "She's not my type." Again, he glanced at Claudia.

Claudia's heart began to beat faster.

"Well, she sure likes you," Jennifer said.

"Look…" John finally turned his full attention to his sister. "Don't encourage her, okay?"

"*Moi?* I wouldn't do that."

"Good."

"No, seriously, John, I *wouldn't* do that."

"I know."

"Well, whatever the reason, we're glad you're here," Jennifer said. "So why don't you make yourself useful and dress the salad—it's in the fridge—while Claudia sets the table?"

Claudia watched John as he confidently drizzled olive oil and vinegar on the salad Jennifer had prepared earlier. He didn't measure, just poured, then he shook in salt and pepper, tossed the mixture and tasted it. He added a bit more salt, then followed it with another taste.

"You know," Jennifer said when he was finished, "you should've gone to culinary school." She placed a large bowl of spaghetti and meatballs in the middle of the table.

"I think about that sometimes," he said.

"But you love what you do," Claudia said.

John grinned. "I know. I'm greedy. I want everything." He picked up the loaf of bread. "Want me to slice this?"

"Yes," Jennifer said. She removed a container of light margarine from the refrigerator and plopped it on the table. "Okay, that's it. Hurry up with that bread,

John. We're hungry." She grinned at Claudia. "Men are so *slow,* aren't they?"

While they ate, they talked about all kinds of things: John's project at work, Jennifer's job woes, Claudia's growing love affair with Houston, then John said, "I moved into my new apartment today."

"Oh, I forgot!" Jennifer said.

Claudia had just finished the last bite of her pasta. She leaned back in her chair. "Did all your furniture get delivered?"

He smiled across the table. "Yeah, and it looks great." Turning to his sister, he said, "Did Claudia tell you she helped me pick out my living room furniture?"

"No, she didn't."

Claudia saw the sudden curious look on Jennifer's face, and she used every ounce of willpower she possessed to keep her own expression from revealing the sudden knot of tension in her belly.

"He got some really nice stuff," she said offhandedly, just as if it were an everyday kind of thing that she would go shopping with him and no big deal at all.

"I can't wait to see it," Jennifer said. "Maybe I'll come by tomorrow after dinner at the folks'. Or do you have something planned?"

"The only thing I plan to do is watch the Texans' game on TV."

Claudia's stomach unknotted as the moment when

Jennifer might have questioned the shopping trip and the reasons behind it passed.

"I've decided I'm going to have a party to christen the apartment," John said. "You're both invited."

"Well," Jennifer said, laughing, "I should hope *so*."

They continued talking for another half hour, then Jennifer got up and began clearing off the table. Claudia finished her wine and rose to help at the same time John did. The three of them made short work of the cleanup. When they were done, Claudia looked at her watch. It was nearly ten. "I should be going," she said. "It's been a long day, and I'm tired."

"Me, too," Jennifer said. She turned to John, "We've been on the go since noon."

"Okay, I can take a hint. I'm outta here, too."

After saying their goodbyes, Claudia and John walked outside together. She couldn't help but be aware of how natural it felt to be with him, and how much she wished they were *really* together. If they had been…but no, she had to put that thought out of her mind.

"Well, good night," she said, reaching for the handle of her car door.

"Good night." He started to say something else when a phone rang.

Claudia thought it was her phone and reached into her purse, but before she could get it out, John was saying hello on his cell.

"Oh, hey, hi, Phil."

Claudia swallowed. She turned away so John couldn't read her expression in the glow from the streetlight.

"I'm just leaving Jen's." After a moment or two of listening, he said, "Yeah, sure. Where do you want to meet?"

A few seconds later, the conversation over, he disconnected the call and put the cell back in his pocket. "That was Philip."

"So I gathered."

"He's on his way home from the game. We're gonna meet for a beer." He smiled. "I'd invite you to come along, but I know you're tired."

"Exhausted." Wild horses couldn't have dragged her along.

"Well, good night again, then. Be careful driving home. Watch for the crazies. There are always a lot of them out on Saturday nights."

"I will." Their gazes met again and Claudia could feel that invisible current of awareness arcing between them. The moment stretched, pregnant with unspoken desire. She knew he wanted to kiss her as much as she wanted to be kissed.

She almost yielded to the urge to put her hands on either side of his head and draw his head down to meet hers. Somehow she found the strength to resist, to instead open the door of her Jeep. Her hands trembled.

"Lock your doors," he said as she climbed in.

"I will." Her voice sounded normal. How could that be, when inside she felt like a total mess?

As she backed out of the driveway, he stood there watching her. He was still watching when she lost sight of him as she turned the corner.

John had wanted to yank her into his arms and kiss her senseless. He'd wanted it so badly he was sure she'd known what he was feeling and that she wanted the same thing. For one crazy minute, John thought she was going to make the first move. If she had, he would have cast every resolution he'd made about staying away from her out the window.

He still couldn't get over how fate seemed to be throwing them together. And the more he saw of her, the more he knew Phil would never get to first base with her.

John swore.

He'd have to tell his cousin about tonight. No way he couldn't, because Jen might mention the evening, and then what? Phil would be upset that he'd missed seeing Claudia. That her plans had changed, and she'd been in town when he'd thought she'd gone home for the weekend.

Had her plans changed, though? Or had she just said she was going home because she didn't want to go out with Phil?

Not that it mattered. The end result was the same.

When John reached Charlie's, a sports bar near

Phil's place, Phil's Explorer was already in the parking lot. John parked, locked his truck, and went inside.

The place was noisy. The after-game Rockets crowd was already there. The big-screen TV was tuned to one of the ESPN channels and was showing the Lakers' game. John saw Phil sitting at the bar and walked over to join him.

"How was the game?" he said, sliding onto a bar stool next to his cousin.

Phil smiled. "We won." He went on to describe a couple of outstanding plays. "So what did you do tonight?"

"I stayed at the apartment until six. That's when the TV delivery people finally showed up."

Phil shook his head. "I guess you should consider yourself lucky they got there today at all."

"Yeah."

"The complex has cable, right?"

"Yep. I'm all set up. More than a hundred channels."

"What can I getcha?" Charlie, the owner and bartender, said to John.

John named a light beer.

"You hungry?" Phil said.

"Nah, I ate at Jen's. I called her to see if she wanted to go for Tex-Mex but she was already fixing dinner and asked me to come over. Guess who else was there," he said as nonchalantly as he could manage.

Phil's even blue gaze met his. "Who?"

"Claudia."

Phil blinked. "Claudia? But I thought she was going home for the weekend. That's what she told me."

"She mentioned that she'd intended to, but I guess she changed her mind."

The look on Phil's face smote John's heart. Dammit, he hated to see his cousin hurting like this.

I wish I'd never met her. I wish she wanted to be with you. If I could change things, I would.

And at that moment, he really felt he would. Because no matter how much he wanted Claudia himself, he could never have her.

So why not make Phil happy?

The first thing Claudia did when she got home that night was check her e-mail. She smiled when she saw Sally's name in her in-box. She double clicked to open the post.

Hey Claudia,
I'm dying to know what's been happening (or not happening) with the whole John/Philip thing. I tried to call you earlier today but got your voice mail. Then when I tried your cell, I got your voice mail there, too. Where have you been? And why didn't you call me back?

I was thinking about coming down next weekend. Would that work for you? If you get this e-mail before eleven, give me a call. Otherwise, we'll touch

base tomorrow. Wherever you've been, I hope you've been having fun!
TTYL, XXXOOO
Sally

Claudia looked at the time. It was after eleven. She didn't really feel like talking to Sally, anyway. Easier to just zap off an e-mail.

She started a new post, telling Sally that she'd love to have her come for the weekend and filling her in on what she'd been doing all day. At the end, she gave her directions for how to find her place in Houston, then sent the post and turned off her computer.

Later, as she lay in bed, she kept thinking about the day—its revelations and its conclusion.

She kept thinking about the look in John's eyes as they stood by her car. How she'd felt he wanted to kiss her and how she'd wanted him to.

And now John and Philip were together. Were they talking about her? Had John told Philip about the evening? What was Philip thinking?

But there were no answers to any of these questions, just as there was no answer to the bigger question of how, through no fault of her own, she had gotten herself into this mess.

Chapter Seven

After saying goodbye to John, Philip headed for home. He had been feeling down ever since John told him about Claudia staying in town over the weekend. Why hadn't she called him if her plans had changed?

You can't blame this on her. You should have told her to call you if for some reason she didn't go out of town. You dropped the ball the way you usually do. If John had been in your shoes, he would have covered his bases. Next time maybe you'll know better.

What was she doing now? he wondered. Was she still awake? What would she say if he just happened call or drop by?

Don't be ridiculous. It's midnight. You can't just

*call or drop by someone's house at midnight, espe-
cially someone like Claudia.*

Even as he told himself this was a crazy idea, Philip
found himself turning the car around and heading toward her condo. He would just see if she was still
awake. If her lights were off, he'd go home. If they
were on, he'd consider his options.

Ten minutes later, he was parked across the street
from her complex. From his vantage point he could see
her unit clearly. The downstairs was dark, but upstairs
there was still a light on. What was she doing? Was she
watching television, maybe in bed? He imagined what
she'd look like propped against her pillows. He would
give anything to be there beside her.

He knew what he was doing was stupid. He was act-
ing like some kind of lovesick high school kid who drives
by his sweetheart's house just to be close to her. *If anyone saw you, they'd think you were some kind of stalker.*

Philip sighed. He wasn't going to ring her doorbell
or throw stones at her window. Maybe guys like John
could do impetuous, romantic things, but guys like him
couldn't get away with stunts like that. Claudia would
just think he was weird. She'd be even less enthusiastic about dating him than she was now.

Because he had to face it.

She wasn't eager to see him again. If she had been,
she wouldn't keep turning him down, no matter *how*
busy she was.

What was wrong with him? Why did he keep having such a problem with women? What was it about him that turned them off? He did everything the experts said to do. He treated them with courtesy and respect. He took them nice places, he bought them appropriate gifts, he complimented them, and he listened.

Supposedly, listening was the key word. And he did. He never monopolized the conversation or talked about himself too much.

And yet the only two women he'd ever been seriously interested in had chosen something—or someone—else over him. Leslie, his first real love, had fallen for a co-worker and dumped Philip after they'd been seeing each other steadily for months and he was beginning to think about marriage. And Emily, to whom he'd actually been engaged, had wanted the job in London more than she'd wanted him.

Just then, Claudia's upstairs window went dark, and Philip knew she was ready for sleep. It was foolish for him to keep sitting there. And yet he couldn't seem to leave.

Lost in his thoughts, he didn't see the police cruiser until the flashing lights were right behind him.

His heart jumped. *Damn!*

Philip told himself to be calm. His mind raced. He knew the officer would want to know what he was doing parked there. Taking a deep breath, he lowered his window as the cop approached.

Act like nothing's wrong. "Hi," he said, forcing a chuckle. "I know I wasn't speeding."

"May I see your driver's license and registration, please?"

Oh, boy. "Certainly." Philip fished them both out of his wallet and handed them to the cop. "What's wrong, officer?" *What if Claudia should happen to look out her window and see him here?* The thought sent chills down his spine.

The cop didn't respond, just shone a small flashlight on the documents, then looked at Philip, then back at the picture on the license. After agonizing minutes that seemed like hours to Philip, the cop finally handed the license and registration back.

"What are you doing here, Mr. Larkin?" he asked.

Philip knew the best defense was a good offense and even though he was scared and embarrassed and mad at himself, he didn't let it show. "Was I breaking some kind of law or something?"

"Please answer the question."

"I was on my way home and my car stalled. When I tried to get it started, it flooded. I was just sitting here waiting before trying again. Is that against the law?"

The cop stared at him. Seconds went by. Finally he said, "No, that's not against the law. But why don't you try to start your car again?"

Philip knew if he put his foot on the gas first, then turned the key in the ignition, it wouldn't start right away. So that's what he did. The second attempt he left his foot off the gas, and it started right up. "Seems okay now. Guess I sat here long enough."

"I guess you did."

"Well, I'll be on my way, then."

The cop nodded. "You do that."

Philip's hands were trembling as he drove off. Thank God Claudia's window had remained dark. Because if she'd happened to see him, Philip would never have been able to face her again.

When John arrived at his parents' house Sunday afternoon, everyone else was already there.

"Am I late?" he said, walking into the living room where his father, his uncle Paul and Phil were all watching the Texans' game.

"No," said his uncle, getting up to shake his hand. "We just got here."

"Game been on long?"

"It's almost halftime," Phil said.

"We winning or losing?"

"Score's tied," said his dad.

After going out to the kitchen to greet his mother, aunt and sister, John took a Coke out of the refrigerator and rejoined the men in the living room. He watched the game halfheartedly. Every once in a while, he'd glance at Phil, who was awfully quiet.

John hoped nothing was wrong. He tried to think

of a reason to get Phil alone but could come up with nothing. For a moment he regretted giving up smoking, a habit he'd tried on briefly back in college. At least that would have given him an excuse to ask his cousin to join him outside.

He was still trying to think of a way to get in a private word with Philip when his mother appeared in the doorway. "Okay, you men. Dinner's ready."

"Perfect timing," said John's dad. "Halftime just started."

"Like I care," she retorted.

"C'mon, tell the truth," John's dad said, "You planned the timing to coincide with halftime." He looked around at the others. "She'd do anything to make me happy, you know."

"You wish." But she was laughing now.

John's dad walked over, put his arm around her and nuzzled her neck. "She can't resist me."

She swatted at him. "Stop that, Lou."

He laughed.

John liked the way his parents fooled around and teased each other. He had always hoped he'd have a relationship like theirs some day. At the rate he was going, though, he'd be eighty before that happened.

If it *ever* happened.

Claudia's image appeared, as it was doing more and more of late. He tried to push it away, but it stubbornly stuck there, taunting him.

Once everyone was seated, his Aunt Margie said the blessing. Then they began to pass the food. Today's dinner consisted of John's mother's oven-baked chicken and corn-bread dressing. His aunt Margie had brought a green-bean casserole and a tossed salad to go with it. And John's dad had baked his specialty—focaccia bread.

Once everyone's plate was full and they'd begun eating, John's mother said, "So what have you young folks been up to this week?"

"Well, I got moved into my new apartment yesterday," John said.

"I wondered about that," his mother said. "When are we going to get invited over to see it?"

"I saw it yesterday," Phil said. "It's nice."

"And I'm going over later today," Jen said.

"Maybe we'll all go," his dad said.

John shrugged. "Sure, why not?"

"So what about you, Jen?" Linda asked. "What did you do yesterday?"

"I had the most fun day," Jen said, smiling. "I met Phil's new girlfriend for lunch and then we went shopping and—"

"Phil's new girlfriend?" John's aunt Margie said. "Philip! You didn't tell me you were dating anyone."

"I wouldn't exactly call her my girlfriend," he said, face flushing.

"Oh, c'mon," Jen said. "Anyone can see how much you like her."

John would have kicked his sister under the table if he could have reached her.

"What's her name? Do I know her?" Phil's mother said.

"No, Mom," Phil said, "you don't know her. She's a teacher at the college. And she's *not* my girlfriend."

"Whatever," Jen said, rolling her eyes. "Anyway, he brought her to my birthday party, and we just hit it off. Don't *you* think she's nice, John?"

"Very," he said uncomfortably.

"Well, tell us about her," Phil's mother pressed. She was smiling. "At least tell us her name."

John knew how much his aunt had hoped Phil would meet someone else ever since Emily had chosen a transfer to her company's London office over her engagement to Phil. Aunt Margie had been heartsick on Phil's behalf, for she had thought the world of Emily, too.

"I'll tell you about her if Phil's too shy," Jen said. "Her name is Claudia. Claudia Hathaway. She's tall and blond and really pretty. And she's lots of fun. I like her a lot. Yesterday, after shopping, she came back to the house and we had dinner together. Actually, John was there, too."

"Why weren't *you* there?" John's aunt said, looking at Phil.

"I went to the Rockets game with Dan Greavy," Phil mumbled.

There was definitely something bugging him, John decided. Something more than what John had told him last night, for he hadn't been that upset when they'd parted to go their separate ways. But what could have happened between then and now? Surely he hadn't called Claudia this morning. Or had he?

"I was only there because I called Jen," John said, belatedly realizing he should explain, "and asked her if she wanted to get something to eat with me. She invited me over then."

"I wish Phil *had* been there," Jen said. She turned to him. "We'll get together another time, the four of us. Or, if John and I can get dates, there'll be six of us."

John watched Phil's face. He smiled at Jen but John could see his heart wasn't in it. Something must *really* be wrong, something more than just knowing Claudia hadn't gone home for the weekend.

Phil's mother smiled at him. "Honey, why don't you bring her to dinner next Sunday? It would give your dad and me and Aunt Linda and Uncle Lou a chance to meet her, too."

"Mom," Phil said, "I told you. We've only had a couple of dates."

"Aunt Margie," Jen said hurriedly, "I shouldn't have said Claudia was Phil's girlfriend. I was just teasing him, that's all."

If she *did* eventually come for dinner some Sunday,

John would find somewhere else to be. No matter how much he liked being around Claudia, he knew he'd have a hard time handling being around her with his entire family watching.

"How long has this Claudia been teaching at the college?" Phil's dad asked.

"She's new this year," Phil said.

"Is she a Houston girl?" his mom asked.

"No, she's from some little town in the hill country."

"What's the name of it, do you know?" Jen asked. "I asked her at lunch yesterday, but then we got sidetracked and I never did find out what it was."

"I don't think she's ever said," Phil said. "I think it's a really small place."

"You know," John's dad said, "years ago I toured the Hathaway Bakery main plant in Morgan Creek. That's a real small town about an hour southwest of Austin. Is she one of those Hathaways, do you think?"

"I don't think so, Dad," Phil said. "They're wealthy, aren't they?"

"Very," Lou Renzo said.

"If she was one of those Hathaways, what would she be doing teaching?" Jen said.

But John wondered. Was it possible? Could Claudia be a wealthy heiress? He thought about the way she talked, the way she looked. It was obvious to anyone with eyes that she was not just intelligent, but cultured and polished.

And yet…if she *were* one of those Hathaways, why *would* she be teaching?

He thought about their conversation at Jen's birthday party and again over coffee after the furniture shopping expedition. And last night she'd talked again about how much she loved teaching.

If she *was* one of those Hathaways, maybe the explanation of why she was teaching was just as simple as she'd said it was: she hated working in the business world.

Poor Phil, if it were true.

He might as well quit torturing himself and throw in the towel right now. Wealthy girls from prominent families might pass the time with men like Phil, but they rarely married them. In fact, John couldn't imagine it happening.

She wouldn't marry anyone like you, either!

If John hadn't already known a relationship with Claudia was not in the cards, he knew it now.

"You know what I did last night?"

John frowned. "You mean after we left Charlie's?" He and Phil were sitting out on John's patio. The rest of the family members had left after a brief tour of the apartment, but Phil had stayed on. It was obvious he wanted to talk.

"Yeah. After we parted company."

"Didn't you go home?"

"I started to, but I ended up driving to Claudia's and sitting across the street from her place for more than an hour."

John stared at his cousin. "Doing what?"

"Just sitting there. Watching her place. Like some kind of stupid kid."

John didn't know what to say.

"I haven't told you the worst part, though."

"She saw you?"

"Worse than that. A cop came by and wanted to know what I was doing there."

"Jesus."

"Yeah. Scared the you-know-what out of me. I didn't even see him until he pulled up behind me."

John listened without comment as Phil told him about the episode. When he was finished, John said, "Well, it could have been worse. Claudia could have seen the whole thing. Then you'd really be embarrassed. As it is, the only thing that happened is you got hassled."

Phil stared into space. "What happened was humiliating." He turned back to John and his eyes were agonized. "What's wrong with me? Why is it that every woman I've ever cared about doesn't seem to care about me?"

"Ah, c'mon, Phil. That's not true."

"Yes, it is. Tell me the truth. What am I doing wrong?"

"Have you ever thought that maybe nothing is wrong *with* you? That maybe the entire problem is due to the fact that you choose women who are completely wrong *for* you."

"What do you mean?"

"I mean you choose women who are too different, who want different things." Now that he'd started, John decided to keep going. Maybe it would help Phil to hear the truth, at least as John saw it. "Take Leslie, for instance. I knew from the beginning you two wouldn't last."

Philip frowned. "Why not?"

"Because she wasn't satisfied with just one man's attention. She put the moves on *me,* a couple of times, and I figured if she'd do that with *me,* she was probably doing it with other guys."

"You never told me that."

"I know. At the time I figured you wouldn't believe me."

"And Emily? You think *she* was wrong for me, too?"

"How can you even ask, after what she did? Hell, Phil, you had blinders on when it came to Emily. She made no bones about what she wanted out of life, but you refused to see the truth."

"All right, maybe you're right, maybe I *did* pick the wrong women before. But Claudia isn't like them. She's different. She's our kind of people. She and I have everything in common."

John didn't say anything for a moment.

"What?" Phil said.

John shrugged. "Nothing. I just—"

"What? Spit it out. What is it about Claudia that's so wrong for me?"

John could see he'd made Phil mad. *Why did you start this? Why didn't you just listen and say nothing? You knew you couldn't win, that if you told him the truth, he'd eventually blame you. It's that old 'shoot the messenger' thing.* "I just wonder…what do you really know about her?"

"What do you mean? What's to know? She's a teacher, she comes from a small town, she has a family she cares about, she's obviously educated and intelligent. Everyone likes her, including you and Jen. She's perfect."

"No one's perfect," John said mildly. But maybe Claudia was actually *too* perfect. Way out of *both* their leagues. He sighed heavily. "Okay, let's say she *is* perfect for you. Then my advice is to cool it a little. Maybe she's just not ready for a relationship, and if you push, you'll blow your chances with her for good. Tell you what, why don't you ask Jen to invite you and me and Claudia over for dinner or something this weekend? Maybe to play games like we used to."

The last thing John wanted was to be around Claudia and Phil, but hadn't he vowed he'd change things for Phil if he could? This was his chance to prove he was sincere.

He plowed doggedly on. "And then I'll have a christening party for the apartment the following weekend. That way you can spend time with Claudia in an easy, relaxed way where she won't feel any pressure. And in the meantime, you can ask her out for something midweek, something different, like ice-skating at that new rink in Memorial City."

"I can't ice-skate."

"Oh, hell, Phil, who cares? She probably can't ice-skate, either. The whole point is to ask her to do something so different she won't say no."

Phil nodded. "Okay. I'll try it. Anything's better than what I've *been* doing."

Claudia didn't see Philip all day Monday. She hoped that meant he was in meetings or otherwise occupied because she had a couple of student files that needed to be returned to the main office and she really didn't want to run into him. Unfortunately, his office was right next door, so sometimes he was hard to avoid.

As luck would have it, Sarah Frost, Philip's secretary, and Philip were standing talking outside the administration office when Claudia approached.

Philip turned. His eyes lit up when he saw her. "Hi, Claudia. Classes over for the day?"

"Yes, all done. I wanted to return these files before I left in case someone needed them."

"I'll take them for you," Sarah said.

"Thanks. Well, see you tomorrow," Claudia said. She turned to go.

"Claudia, wait. I, uh, was going to come down to your classroom. Can we, uh, talk for a minute?"

Claudia sighed inwardly. She'd thought she was going to escape without having to dodge another invitation from Philip. "Sure."

Once they were out of Sarah's earshot, Philip smiled. "You look awfully pretty today."

"Thanks."

"John told me you and Jen spent Saturday together. I guess that means you changed your mind about going home."

"Yes, it didn't work out. But I had a great day with Jennifer." Claudia looked at her watch. "Look, I'm kind of in a hurry. I, um, have a doctor's appointment."

He frowned. "Oh, sorry. I hope it's nothing serious."

"No, just a routine visit." Oh, God. Why did she have to say that about a doctor? When would she learn that the less said, the better?

"Well, I won't keep you. I just wanted to say I'm glad you and Jen are becoming friends."

As Claudia walked away, she wondered why he hadn't asked her out again. She knew he'd wanted to. And yet he hadn't. Hope flared. Had he finally realized she wasn't interested?

She crossed her fingers, almost afraid to keep the

hope alive, as if doing so would jinx any chance it had of being justified.

But no matter how she cautioned herself, she felt happier and more optimistic about the Philip/John situation than she'd felt in weeks.

Chapter Eight

Claudia had just polished off a Lean Cuisine entrée, a glass of milk and some strawberries when her phone rang. She recognized Jennifer's number.

"Hi, Jennifer!"

"Hi, Claudia. I didn't get you in the middle of anything, did I?"

"Just finished dinner." She wondered if she would like Jennifer as much if she wasn't John's sister. Yet even as Claudia asked herself this, she knew she would have wanted Jennifer as a friend under any circumstances.

"I just wanted to say again how much I enjoyed spending the day with you on Saturday," Jennifer said.

"Ditto."

"And I was wondering what your plans are for the weekend. Or if you have any."

"My friend Sally's coming."

"The one from Austin?"

"Uh-huh. She'll be here about five on Friday."

"What will you do on Friday night?"

"I don't know. In fact, I was going to call *you,* see if you wanted to do something with us."

"That's perfect, then, because I called to invite you to come over Friday for a game night. I'm planning to ask John and Philip, as well, and maybe this guy at work that I kind of like. Do you think Sally would enjoy something like that?"

It *did* sound like fun, and even though Philip would be there, John would be, too. And she wouldn't be on a date. She and Sally would arrive together and leave together. It was perfect. Sally would get to meet both John *and* Philip, as well as Jennifer. "I think it sounds great, and I know Sally would enjoy it."

"Oh, good. I'll tell the guys to come at seven, but why don't you and Sally come around six? That way we'll have a chance to get in some girl talk before they arrive."

"All right. Can I bring anything? Chips and dips? Wine?"

"Chips and some kind of dip would be nice. Otherwise, I'll have it under control. I'm taking Friday off—

actually, I have an interview Friday morning. Anyway, I thought I'd fix a big pot of chili and a salad for dinner, but I hadn't thought about a snack. And knowing the guys, they'll probably want one once dinner wears off."

"Okay. Now tell me about the interview. When did this happen?"

"Remember on Saturday when I said I'd sent a résumé to the classic-rock radio station?"

"Yeah."

"Well, the station manager called me this morning. He's looking for an assistant, and he wants to talk to me about the job."

"Oh, that's great. Good luck."

"Thanks."

"Now what about that *guy?* I didn't think—" Claudia broke off.

"Didn't think what?"

Claudia hesitated, then decided to take the plunge. "I hope you don't mind, but Philip told me about your fiancé, and…well…he said you weren't dating yet."

"No, I don't mind. And I'm not dating. But I think I'm finally ready to." Her voice thickened. "I loved Matt with all my heart. I'll always love him. But I can't live on a memory forever."

"No."

"And Riley, well, he's such a sweetheart. A really nice, kind man. I think…I think I could care for him.

But he doesn't seem to think of me in that way. I mean, so far we're just buddies, you know?"

"And you'd like to change that?"

"Maybe. Friday night will be an experiment. If he says yes, that is."

Claudia thought about how pretty and smart and nice Jennifer was. If this Riley had any brains at all, he'd jump at the chance to spend an evening with her. "What does this Riley do?"

"He's the head writer for the station's five and six o'clock news."

"Does he have a first name?"

Jennifer laughed. "Riley *is* his first name. Riley Peterson."

"Well, I'm looking forward to meeting him. And to Friday night. Thanks for thinking of it."

"So can you come?"

Wild horses wouldn't have kept John away if Claudia was going to be there. *So much for your resolutions.* "Sure, sounds like fun."

"Great. Now I'm going to call Phil," his sister said. "Oh, and just so you won't be surprised, I'm inviting a friend of mine from work."

"Anyone I know?"

"Uh-uh. He's a writer I've worked with quite a bit. His name is Riley Peterson."

John's antennae perked up. A man? His sister was

interested in a man? "Something I should know about this Riley?"

"Don't get ideas. We're just friends, that's all."

John thought she'd protested much too quickly. Which told him everything he needed to know. He was glad he'd get a chance to check out this Riley, see if he was good enough for Jennifer, but even if he wasn't, John was still glad to see his sister was finally coming back to the land of the living. Matt had been a great guy, one John would have been proud to have as a brother-in-law, but Matt was dead, and Jennifer wasn't.

John knew his parents concurred. None of them wanted Jennifer to spend the rest of her life grieving over what might have been. John's mom wanted grandchildren, she wanted both her kids to marry and be happy. Not that marriage guaranteed happiness. Far from it, John thought, but he knew where his mother was coming from. He wanted his sister to be happy, too.

"Okay, sis, no ideas," he said. "I'll see you on Friday. Hope your interview goes okay."

Philip smiled when he hung up the phone. John had come through for him. He'd obviously talked to Jennifer and arranged this whole game-night idea.

He thought about the rest of John's advice. To invite Claudia to do something unusual, something she wouldn't say no to. Should he do it after the game night and before John's party? Or wait until after the party?

Well, he had plenty of time to decide.

In the meantime, he'd continue to give Claudia space. He felt encouraged that John's plan might work because she seemed friendlier now than she had before, more inclined to want to spend a few minutes talking to him when they saw each other in the halls or when she had to come to the administration offices.

If this works, I'll be the one in John's debt, not the other way around.

Philip had always felt uncomfortable knowing that his cousin *did* feel indebted to him. Philip hadn't given John a kidney because he wanted thanks. He'd done it because it was the right thing to do, and he knew if their positions had been reversed, John would have come through for him in an instant.

They hadn't always had a perfect relationship. Philip had been envious of John many times, had even felt resentment toward him—sometimes he still did— and he was sure John had had some negative feelings toward and about him, too. Hell, they were both human.

But they were also bonded by blood. Double cousins. Almost as close as if they were siblings.

You might resent your brother, you might even hate him at times. But in the end, he was your brother.

* * *

For the rest of the week, Claudia looked forward to Friday night. On Friday afternoon, she left school shortly after three and made it home by three forty-five, well ahead of Sally's expected arrival.

Deciding she had time for a shower, Claudia raced upstairs, stripped off her clothes, and was in and out of the shower in less than ten minutes.

Thirty minutes later, hair moussed and dried, dressed in army-green cargo pants and a matching three-quarter sleeved skinny T-shirt, her clogs, and the ever-present armful of bracelets, Claudia checked to make sure there were clean towels and a new bar of soap in the guest bath, and that the guest room looked inviting.

Satisfied everything was ready for Sally, Claudia headed back downstairs to get herself something cold to drink while she checked her e-mail.

She was still reading and replying to messages when her doorbell rang. Glancing at her watch, she saw it was only four-thirty. Sally had made good time.

"Claudia!" Sally said when Claudia opened the door, "I *love* your place."

"You haven't even seen it yet," Claudia pointed out, laughing.

"I mean the whole complex. It's gorgeous." Sally put her overnight bag down and hugged Claudia hard.

"C'mon, I'll show you around."

Sally oohed and aahed over Claudia's furniture and the layout of the condo, and kept a mile-a-minute monologue going in between, telling Claudia how her mother was driving her crazy and how her sister Kristin was thinking of getting a divorce and how their mutual friend Bart had suffered a broken collarbone in an accident the day before.

"Whoa, slow down," Claudia said.

"Can't help it. I've missed talking to you."

"Sally, we've talked every other night since I moved here."

"I know, but it's not the same."

Claudia couldn't help laughing. "It's *exactly* the same. Talk is talk, no matter where the parties live."

"No, it's not. The thing is, *I* know you're *here* and not in Morgan Creek. That makes a difference."

Claudia was still shaking her head over Sally's logic—which actually made a weird kind of sense to Claudia—as she led the way to the guest room. While Sally unpacked, Claudia told her about the evening's plans.

"Oh, that sounds like fun!" Sally said. "I'm dying to meet Philip and John."

"I figured you would be."

"How long will it take us to get there?"

"No more than fifteen minutes."

"Then I have time to freshen up?"

Claudia waited downstairs until Sally was ready.

When she came down, Claudia saw she'd changed into cropped khaki pants and a bright red sweater that complemented her dark hair and still-tanned skin.

"Are you going to one of those tanning places?" she asked as they prepared to leave.

"Why?"

"Sally…you know they're bad for you."

"I don't like white skin," Sally mumbled.

"Okay. When you get skin cancer, don't come crying to me."

"Did I lecture *you* when you were smoking?"

Claudia made a face. "Point taken."

Sally continued her earlier chatter during the short drive to Jennifer's, mostly giving Claudia the rundown on what had happened to Kristen's and Bill's marriage that was threatening to put it to an end.

"But didn't she *know* how he felt about having kids before they were married?"

Sally shrugged. "I don't know. She says she didn't, but I think she just figured he didn't mean it and she'd change his mind."

"Marriage is such an iffy proposition, isn't it?" Claudia mused. She was thinking about her brother Bryce and how his beloved first wife, Michelle, had died. And about Lorna and how her husband had had an affair with his assistant. And, of course, about her own parents, who were still together but obviously miserable with each other.

And yet…there *were* good marriages, too. Her oldest sister Chloe had a great marriage, and from what John and Jennifer had told her, their parents did, too.

"I know you take a chance when you get married," Sally said, "but I still hope I do. Of course," she added dryly, "I'll have to *find* someone first."

"Yeah. Me, too."

"Seems to me you *have* found someone. Two someones. And I'm excited that I'm going to get to meet them both tonight."

"I'll be curious to see what you think. Oh, and I almost forgot. Please don't say anything about my family. I haven't said anything about them, and I'd like to keep it that way for a while."

"Do you think Philip and John and Jennifer would change toward you if they knew?"

"I don't know. I'd just rather wait until we've been friends longer."

"Claudia, you're paranoid when it comes to your family, you know that?"

"Maybe." But Sally hadn't had to contend with the fawning, the not-so-subtle bid for favors, the requests for money and the ill-disguised resentment when she refused. "But it's been my experience that people just look at me differently when they know my background." *And they realize how much money I'm likely to inherit.*

Sally only nodded, and a few minutes later, Claudia pulled up in front of Jennifer's house, so the subject was dropped. Claudia would have parked in the driveway, but she didn't want to get blocked in just in case the situation became uncomfortable or something and she needed to make a quick getaway.

A smiling Jennifer opened the door. Claudia made the introductions and watched as her two friends sized each other up.

"You're just like Claudia described you," Jennifer said.

"So are you," Sally said.

They both grinned.

Claudia breathed a sigh of relief. She could tell they'd get along fine.

"C'mon back," Jennifer said. "You two can have a glass of wine and talk to me while I finish making the salad."

"Mmm, smells good," Claudia said as they entered the kitchen. She eyed the pot on the stove. "Can I peek?"

Jennifer smiled. "Sure, go ahead. Why don't you stir while you're at it? In the meantime, I'll pour y'all some wine. Red okay? I've still got some of that Shiraz."

They both said the Shiraz was fine.

Claudia lifted the lid on the pot of chili. "This looks so good." She picked up the wooden spoon Jennifer had obviously been using and stirred. "Is that bits of jalapeño pepper I see in there?"

"Uh-huh. Not too much, though. Some people don't like their food real hot."

She handed Sally and Claudia their glasses of wine, then resumed making her salad, which looked about halfway done. Sally perched on a bar stool and Claudia leaned against the counter, watching.

"So how was your drive in?" Jennifer asked Sally.

"I made good time. The traffic wasn't too bad, which surprised me. I thought Friday afternoons on 290 were always heavy."

"You were lucky," Claudia said. The last trip she'd made to Morgan Creek had taken her an hour longer than usual. "But Jennifer, tell us about the job interview. How'd it go?"

Jennifer grinned. "I got the job."

"*Really?* That's wonderful!"

"Yeah, I'm tickled."

Turning to Sally, Claudia said, "Jennifer had an interview this morning."

"So I gathered."

"I want to hear everything," Claudia said.

"Well," Jennifer said, pausing in the midst of cutting up some baby carrots. "First of all, Tom—that's the station manager, Tom Slocum—is just great. I liked everything he said about his philosophy of work, his goals for the station, how he feels about his employees, just everything. He's really nice and super smart."

"Is he cute?" Claudia said.

"If you can call a sixty-year-old balding man cute," Jennifer said with a laugh.

"There's Sean Connery," Sally pointed out.

"He's sexy, but he's not cute," Jennifer said.

"Finish telling us what happened," Claudia said.

"He showed me around, told me what the job would consist of—which sounded like a piece of cake to me after what I've been required to do at the TV station—and then he offered me the job. More money, fewer hours, and better working conditions. What more could a person ask for? Oh, and it's closer to where I live, too."

"When do you start?"

"I plan to give my notice on Monday, so two weeks from then."

"I'm thinking of looking for another job, too," Sally said. She worked as a paralegal in a high-powered Austin law office.

"What is this? A disease?" Claudia said.

Sally shrugged. "I'm tired of the stress. I'll tell ya, working this job did *one* good thing for me. It cured me of the idea I might like to become a lawyer myself."

"So you don't want to be a paralegal at all anymore?" Claudia asked.

Sally shook her head.

"What will you do instead?" Claudia couldn't voice what she really wanted to say, which was, *What else are you qualified to do?*

"You know how my grandmother made me the beneficiary of her insurance policy?"

"Yes."

"Well, I was going to save the money and use it as a down payment on a house."

"Yeah, and I thought that was a good plan."

"I can still do that, just with a smaller down payment. I thought I'd use the rest to stake me while I start my own business."

"Really?" Jennifer and Claudia said at the same time.

"What kind of business?" Claudia said.

"Web design. Maybe even get my certification to work on personal computers. You know, go out to homes and help people who are having problems with theirs and who don't know what to do."

Claudia thought about that for a moment. "You know, that's a great idea, Sally. You've done a fantastic job with Bill's Web site." Sally's brother-in-law owned a restaurant and Sally had designed his site. "And you're a whiz with computers."

Sally smiled happily.

"I say go for it," Jennifer said. "Life is too darned short to spend it doing something you don't like."

"Amen," Claudia and Sally said together.

The three of them continued to talk as Jennifer finished her preparations. "The guys should be here soon," she said.

The words were barely out of her mouth when the

doorbell rang. Jennifer wiped her hands on her apron, removed it, said, "I'll get it," and blew out of the kitchen like a shot.

Sally grinned at Claudia. "I think she's anxious to see someone."

A few minutes later, a smiling Jennifer brought a big, curly-haired redhead into the kitchen. "This is Riley," she said. Her eyes were shining.

"Hi," he said, ducking his head.

Why, he's shy, Claudia thought, charmed.

"Jennifer tells us you're a brilliant writer," Sally said.

He beamed, turning his warm brown eyes to Jennifer. "Not really brilliant."

And he's definitely interested in her. She just can't see it yet.

The doorbell rang again.

"This time, why don't *you* get it, Claudia?" Jennifer said.

For the second time in a week, Claudia drew in a deep breath while walking toward Jennifer's front door. Her heart had quickened.

Who was on the other side?

John?

Or Philip?

Not that it mattered. Both presented a different set of problems.

Remember, there's safety in numbers.

She took a deep breath, then opened the door.

Chapter Nine

John couldn't remember when he'd had as much fun. For the first time, in both Claudia's and Philip's presence, he felt completely relaxed, just as if there weren't this huge thing going on among them.

It was the games.

Jen had them play on teams, but she wouldn't allow them to choose their teammates. "I think we should play either two teams of three or three teams of two," she said. "What do you guys think?"

They decided on three teams of two, so Jen put six pieces of paper in a cup. Two pieces of paper said *1*, two said *2*, and two said *3*. John and Riley drew the *1*s. Jen and Claudia drew the *2*s. And Sally and Phil drew the *3*s.

"Okay, *partner,*" Sally said, grinning at Phil.

This was interesting, John thought. Sally had been smiling at Phil since he'd arrived. At first John had thought she was just friendly—and she *was*—but for the past hour, he'd begun to think she liked Phil more than normal.

Sally was Claudia's best friend. John knew because Claudia had said so when she'd made the introductions. "Sally and I roomed together all through college. We've been best friends ever since."

"I'm impressed," John had said. "If you're still friends after rooming together."

Claudia laughed. "Well, I didn't say she was perfect."

"Hey, watch it," Sally said. "Anyway, you're not perfect, either."

"I never said I was."

So far, *John* thought Claudia was perfect. And if they were a couple, he would have said so, even though he knew he'd be teased unmercifully afterwards.

So if Sally was Claudia's best friend, she would be sure to know if Claudia was interested in Phil in a romantic way. And she wouldn't be making eyes at him if Claudia *was,* would she?

Throughout Taboo, the game where Phil and Sally were teammates, John watched Phil's reaction to Sally carefully. When they did well and high-fived, when they didn't do well and Sally draped her arm over his shoulder in comradely commiseration, when Sally gave her answers and Phil watched *her,* and vice versa.

And John saw almost at once that Phil responded to Sally. Her exuberance and open admiration drew him out and made him seem more interesting and fun and less reserved.

During the second game—Outburst—they decided to just have two teams. Sally and Phil again ended up on the same team, this time with Jennifer making the third, and John, Riley and Claudia forming the opposition.

And again, the same thing happened. Sally hung on Phil's every word, she cheered every time he scored a point, she patted his arm when he goofed and in general acted as if he were the Game God of All Time, not to mention someone she thought was *wonderful,* which seemed to be her favorite word.

For the first time since he'd found out Phil's new romantic interest was Claudia, the girl of his dreams, John felt hopeful that some day things might work out the way he wanted.

"I think you're crazy, Claudia," Sally said.

"Why?" They were on their way back to Claudia's condo. It was nearly one in the morning.

"Because Philip is *terrific.* He's *wonderful.* Honestly, if he was after me, I'd be *thrilled.*"

"And you *don't* think John is equally wonderful?"

"He's *okay.* I mean, he's cute and all, and I can see why you'd like him—'cause he *is* the type you tend to go for—but Philip is so much more *substantial.* Philip is the kind of man who will make a commitment. John? I don't know. I think he's more the love-'em-for-a-while type, then leave-'em. But hey, it's your life."

"Too bad Philip isn't chasing after *you* then," Claudia said. She knew she sounded irritable, but Sally's comments had stung.

"Anytime you want to steer him my way…"

Later, while Claudia lay in bed and tried to unwind so she could fall asleep, she thought about what Sally had said. She hated to admit it, but Sally was probably right. John *did* seem like the type of guy who might never marry. Even if it hadn't been for the impediment of Philip, maybe Claudia would have been wasting her time mooning over John.

On the other hand, maybe Sally had just been struck by the same love wand that had struck Claudia when she'd met John. The one that made the object of your affections seem perfect and all others pale in comparison.

Anyway, what did Sally's opinion matter?

Claudia knew from past experience that you could not make your heart feel what it didn't feel.

No matter how you might wish you could.

"Last night was lots of fun," Sally said to Jennifer the next afternoon.

"I thought so, too."

Claudia ate some of her popcorn. The three of them were at the Edwards Theater on Weslayan, waiting on the new Nicole Kidman movie to begin.

"What did you think of Riley?" Jennifer asked.

"He's a sweetie," Sally said.

"Do you really think so? What about you, Claudia? Did you like him?"

"I liked him very much. And Jen? He's definitely interested in you. He's just shy."

"Not *that* shy," Jennifer said.

Her tone of voice made Claudia turn and stare at her. "Did he ask you *out?*"

"Uh-huh. After you guys left, he asked me if I wanted to take in a movie or something next Friday."

Sally squealed.

"That's terrific!" Claudia said.

Just then the lights dimmed and the commercials—playing at a decibel level high enough to shatter eardrums—began, so all conversation ended.

When the movie was over, they went to P. F. Chang's for dinner, then ended back at Claudia's for a glass of wine. By the time Jennifer left for home, Claudia was beat, and she and Sally both headed for bed.

On Sunday Sally left after breakfast. She was coming back the next weekend because John had invited her to his party. Again, Claudia was glad for two reasons. She enjoyed having Sally around, and she could once more avoid having to say "no" if Philip wanted to take her to the party as his date.

The day flew by after Sally's departure. Claudia played catch-up on all the things she normally took care of on Saturdays, and before she knew it, it was ten o'clock and time for bed. At heart, Claudia was a night owl, but she knew she needed a good eight hours sleep before a work day.

Monday also flew by. When her classes were over, Claudia went to a hair salon that had been recommended by Jennifer and had the works—haircut, manicure, pedicure and massage.

At six o'clock, feeling fresh and clean and beautifully pampered, she stopped and picked up a low-carb chicken wrap from Subway and headed home.

She was licking her fingers after wolfing down the sandwich when the phone rang.

It was Bryce.

"Hey, Bryce. What's up?"

"I'm afraid I've got some bad news. Dad's had a heart attack."

Shocked speechless, Claudia didn't say anything for a moment. Chill bumps had broken out on her arms. "Oh, no," she finally managed. "Is…is he going to be all right?"

"It doesn't look good. He's in intensive care at the county hospital. Mom wanted him to be taken to Austin, but he's too critical to be moved. I think you'd better come."

Claudia's hands were shaking when she hung up. *Dad.* She sat down. *Dad.* She sat there for long moments. Somehow, despite his drinking, Claudia had imagined her father to be indestructible, the same way her Grandmother Hathaway was. Gran was almost ninety-one. Claudia's father was only sixty-eight.

Tears welled, sliding unchecked down Claudia's face. She allowed herself to cry for a few minutes, then she angrily reached for a tissue. She had learned a long time ago that tears solved nothing.

A moment later, she was punching in Philip's home number. The phone at the other end rang three times before he answered.

"Philip? It's Claudia." She sniffed.

"Claudia? Is something wrong?"

"Yes, I, um…" She took a deep breath. "My father's had a heart attack," she said more firmly. "My brother just called. He said it's pretty serious. Th-they're afraid he won't make it."

"Oh, Claudia, I'm sorry."

"Thank you. Anyway, I'm going to pack some things and drive home tonight. I don't know when I'll be back, but I'll call you tomorrow and let you know."

"Of course. Listen, don't worry about a thing. We'll see that your classes are covered."

"Thank you," she said again.

"And Claudia?"

"Yes?"

"Drive carefully."

"I will. Do you have my cell phone number?"

"No."

She gave it to him. "If you need to reach me, use that number."

An hour later, she was on her way to Morgan Creek.

John disconnected the call and sat quietly thinking. He was glad Phil had thought to call Jen and that his sister had thought to call him. He just wished he had the right to call Claudia and see how she was doing.

Damn.

He didn't even have her cell phone number, and he couldn't very well ask Jennifer for it, although he knew she *did* have it. He supposed Phil had it, too.

I'm the odd man out.

It was at that moment that he knew he loved Claudia. Not just wanted her. Loved her.

He wanted to be there for her when she needed something.

He wanted to take care of her.

"I love her," he whispered.

He had never felt more helpless.

It was after midnight when Claudia finally pulled through the security gates at the family complex in

Morgan Creek. The lights of the main house blazed, and as she approached and entered the front turnaround, the double doors opened and her sister Lorna's silhouette appeared in the doorway.

Claudia stepped out of the Jeep. Lorna came down the steps and they hugged.

"What are you doing here?" Claudia asked. "I thought you'd be at the hospital."

"I was. I came back about thirty minutes ago to wait for you. Let's get your stuff inside, then we'll go back together."

"Okay."

Wanda Janny, their longtime housekeeper, stood in the entryway. Her expression reflected concern. "Miss Claudia," she said. "Would you like me to fix something for you to eat before you go?"

Claudia shook her head. "No, thanks, Mrs. Janny. Do I need to change clothes?" she asked Lorna. She looked down at her jeans and sweater.

"You look fine."

Fifteen minutes later, the sisters were on their way in Lorna's BMW. County General, the hospital that served Morgan Creek and the surrounding area, was only a ten-minute drive from their home.

On the way, Lorna briefed Claudia on what to expect. "He looks awful, so be prepared."

"Is he conscious?"

"Yes, but it was a bad heart attack with a lot of damage. His prognosis isn't good."

Claudia nodded.

When they arrived at the second-floor ICU waiting area, the rest of the family—Claudia's mother and grandmother, her brother Bryce and his wife, Amy, and her oldest sister Chloe—were all there. Claudia went straight to her grandmother, who was sitting. She knelt down in front of her to kiss her cheek and hug her. "How are you doing, Gran?"

Stella Morgan Hathaway, as befitting the strong, dominant woman she'd always been, sat ramrod straight. Her blue eyes—which all of her children had inherited—were dry and unblinking as she regarded her youngest granddaughter. "I'm fine. I'm glad you're here." Unsaid was the inference that Claudia should have been there the whole time. Would have been if she'd listened to her grandmother instead of moving to Houston to begin with.

If Claudia hadn't felt so sad, she might have smiled. Her grandmother would never change. *And I'm glad,* she thought. At least they always knew what to expect.

Next Claudia turned to her mother, who had been standing at the window looking out. Again, as always, Kathleen Bryce Hathaway was impeccably and beautifully dressed and groomed. Every blond hair—kept the exact same color as in her youth by a talented hairdresser—was smoothly drawn back into a chignon.

Her makeup was equally flawless. "Hello, dear," she said, opening her arms to Claudia.

That gesture alone would have alerted Claudia to the seriousness of the situation, for her mother was not given to caresses of any kind. The most her children ever expected was a peck on the cheek. "Mom," she said, holding her mother close. Faint traces of Joy, her mother's favorite perfume, clung to her skin. Claudia wondered at her mother's reaction. Did she still love Claudia's father, then? Is that what this uncharacteristic softness meant?

When her mother released her, Claudia finally had a chance to greet her brother, sister and sister-in-law.

"Any change?" Lorna asked when the greetings were over.

"No," Bryce said.

"When is the next visiting time?"

He glanced at the clock on the wall. "In ten minutes."

"They only allow you to see the patients once every hour for ten minutes," Lorna explained to Claudia. "They won't bend that rule, but they *did* allow all of us to see him when they're only supposed to let two in at a time."

"I should hope *so*," Claudia's grandmother said. "The Hathaways endowed this entire wing."

Claudia bit back a smile. Nope. Gran never changed. She firmly believed rank had its privileges and saw nothing wrong with that.

For the remainder of the ten minutes before they'd be permitted to see Jonathan, the family sat quietly. Lorna reached for Claudia's hand and Claudia gratefully gave it to her. Of all her siblings, Lorna was her favorite, probably because they were closest in age, with Lorna only thirty-three to Claudia's twenty-nine.

The clock on the wall ticked the seconds off loudly. When the hands reached the one o'clock mark, Bryce stood and walked over to the nurses' station. After speaking to the nurse on duty, he gestured to the rest of them.

Claudia took a deep breath as they entered the ICU, which turned out to be a large room with six partitioned sections. Three were empty. Her father was in the last one on the right-hand side, with no one next to him or across from him. Claudia imagined that was the closest thing to privacy that was possible under the circumstances.

The family gathered at the entrance to his section, with Grandmother Stella leaning on Bryce. Claudia's mother urged Claudia forward. "Go ahead," she murmured. "The rest of us have already had our chance to talk to him."

Claudia swallowed. Her heart was beating too fast and her hands felt clammy.

Lorna had been right. Their father looked awful, not like himself at all. Jonathan Morgan Hathaway, despite his love of booze, had always appeared to be healthy, with ruddy skin and clear eyes. He'd inherited a stocky build, a robust laugh and a deep voice from his father—all of which had made him appear to be a strong, confident man, even though he was neither.

Tonight, lying on his hospital bed, attached to what seemed like dozens of wires and machines that beeped and zigged and zagged in living color, he seemed to have shrunk into a man dozens of years older than he actually was.

His eyes were closed, his breathing shallow. An oxygen tank sat nearby, but he didn't seem to be connected to it.

Claudia reached out to touch his left hand. "Dad," she said softly.

His eyes opened slowly. For a moment, they seemed unfocused, then gradually they fastened on to her face. "Claudie…"

Claudia's eyes filled with tears. *Claudie.* It was his baby name for her, one he hadn't used in years. She bent down and kissed him lightly on the cheek. "Daddy," she whispered. Her hand tightened on his. "I love you."

"Love…you…too…" It seemed to take all his strength to get the three words out.

Claudia wanted to weep, yet she knew she had to hold on, not just for his sake, but for her family's, too. She blinked back the tears and used all her willpower to keep her voice steady. Straightening, she said,

"Don't try to talk. You need your strength to get well. I just wanted you to know I'm here."

His eyes told her he was glad.

Later, after the visiting time was over and the family was all once again in the waiting area, Claudia closed her eyes and relived those few minutes she'd spent with her father. She was so grateful her father was still alive and that she'd had a chance to see him and talk to him.

Maybe they'd be lucky.

Maybe he was stronger than the doctors thought or his heart wasn't as damaged as they believed.

Maybe he'd pull through and have many more years to live. Claudia hoped so. She hoped so with all her heart.

The next few hours seemed to crawl by. They all went in to see Jonathan again at two and again at three.

At three-thirty, a white-coated, fortyish physician stepped off the elevator and walked down the hall toward them.

Claudia's mother stood to greet him. "Jim," she said.

"You're still here? I thought I told you to go home."

"That's Dr. Harper, Dad's cardiologist," Bryce said in an aside to Claudia.

Claudia studied the doctor, whose face wore that serious-doctor look she hated.

"Did they call you?" Claudia's mother was asking.

"Yes," Jim Harper said.

"Has something happened?"

"Let me go in and see him. I'll come out and give you a report."

The six of them sat anxiously for the fifteen minutes the cardiologist was gone. When he came out, his face looked even more serious, which Claudia wouldn't have thought possible.

"It's not good," he said. "I don't believe he has much time left."

Claudia bit her lip. She couldn't look at her siblings or her mother or grandmother. She was afraid if she did, she might break down, and she was determined not to because she didn't want to let her grandmother down.

In the end, no matter how much she'd tried to escape the family legacy, she was, after all, a Hathaway.

Jonathan Morgan Hathaway died at four fifty-five that morning. At the end, his mother, wife and children were with him.

No one cried.

But Claudia knew they all felt the same grief and loss, even her mother.

Later, when they waited to speak with Dr. Harper, Claudia saw how Bryce put his arm around Amy, holding her close, and she wished she had someone she loved there to hold *her* close.

Not just someone, she thought. *John*.

She wondered if he knew about her dad. Had Philip called him?

And yet, why would he? Philip didn't know how Claudia felt about John or how—she hoped—John felt about her.

Tomorrow she would call Philip again. And maybe she'd call Jennifer, too. Jennifer, she knew, *would* tell John. Claudia guessed she'd have to be satisfied with that.

But for now she needed to put John out of her mind and focus her thoughts and her energies on her mother and her grandmother and all the decisions that needed to be made.

Chapter Ten

John rarely got up early enough to read the paper before going in to work, but on Wednesday he was rudely awakened by the yowling of two cats who sounded as if they were having a fight to the death right outside his bedroom window.

After chasing them off, he staggered into the kitchen, plugged in the coffeemaker, then headed for the bathroom. Ten minutes later, steaming mug of coffee in hand and marginally awake, he opened his front door to find the *Chronicle* lying on the stoop.

As always, he read the Houston section first, paying particular attention to the film reviews. Next came the sports section, followed by a desultory scan of the main news section. Same old, same old, he thought, putting it on the "finished" pile. He almost skipped the city and state section. As he idly turned the pages, he nearly missed the article because he wasn't paying close attention.

Suddenly, the headline leaped out at him: *Hathaway Baking Company Tycoon Dead At Sixty-Eight.* John stared, then quickly read the article.

Jonathan Morgan Hathaway, 68, son of Stella Morgan Hathaway and the late Richard Jonathan Hathaway, died at County General Hospital in Morgan Creek early Tuesday morning due to complications following a heart attack.

Mr. Hathaway's grandfather, Roland Maxwell Hathaway, founded the company now known as Hathaway Baking Company, Inc., in 1914. It began as a small bakery and has grown into a corporation that now employs more than 5,000 people over the tri-state area of Texas, Oklahoma and Louisiana.

Mr. Hathaway is descended from a long line of distinguished ancestors including his aunt, Claudia Hathaway Richardson, an army nurse during World War II who received the Purple Heart; Roland Morgan Hathaway, a decorated hero who served in the Spanish-American War; and Jonathan Miller Hathaway, who not only founded the town of Morgan Creek, but fought alongside Sam Houston at the Battle of San Jacinto in April 1836.

Mr. Hathaway was, until his retirement, president of the board of directors of the family business.

In addition to his mother, Mr. Hathaway leaves his wife, Kathleen Bryce Hathaway; his son, Jonathan Bryce Hathaway; his daughters, Chloe Hathaway Standish, Lorna Morgan Hathaway and Claudia Elizabeth Hathaway; his son-in-law, Greg Standish; daughter-in-law, Amy Summers Hathaway; and granddaughters, Cameron Kathleen Standish, Stella Ann Hathaway, Susan Adele Hathaway and Calista Hathaway.

Mr. Hathaway was a member of the board of directors of the Morgan Creek Country Club, a member of the church council at Morgan Creek Methodist Church, a member of the board of directors of the Morgan Creek School District, president of the steering committee of the Morgan Bailey Livestock Show and Rodeo, as well as an active contributor to a long list of community projects.

Visitation will take place at Resthaven Funeral Home in Morgan Creek on Thursday from 6:00 to 8:00 p.m. The funeral service will be at 11:00 a.m. Friday at Morgan Creek Methodist

Church, followed by interment at Resthaven Cemetery.

The family requests that any who wish to honor Mr. Hathaway's memory should send a donation to the children's wing at County General Hospital in Morgan Creek or the Food for Needy Families Fund at Morgan Creek Methodist Church.

The article went on to list the pallbearers and give the addresses of the funeral home, the church and the cemetery.

John sank back in his chair. *Whoa.* So what he'd suspected had been true. Claudia was indeed a member of the wealthy Hathaway Baking family.

He wondered if Philip knew.

He reached for his cell phone, almost punched in the speed-dial code for Phil, then changed his mind and called Jennifer instead. He knew she'd be at work. Even now, serving out her notice, she still arrived at the crack of dawn.

"Did you have a chance to see the morning paper?" he asked when she'd answered.

"You mean the article about Claudia's dad?"

"Yeah."

"No, I didn't see it, but we're covering the story on the morning news, so I've gotten all the details."

"Wonder why she didn't tell us who her family was?"

"I've been thinking about that," Jen said, "and I'm sure it has to do with the way people treat her if they know. I imagine she's sick of people sucking up to her."

John guessed his sister might be right. He hadn't considered that aspect before, but now that he had, it made sense. "I'd like to call her, give her my sympathy."

"I'm sure she'd like that. I thought I'd call her, too, after I get home tonight."

"You wouldn't happen to have her cell phone number, would you?"

"Yeah, it's right here." She rattled off the number.

John scrawled it on the margin of the still-open newspaper. "Thanks, Jen. Um, do you think we should send flowers?"

"That's a good idea. Maybe you and I and Phil could go in together? If we did that, we could get a really nice arrangement."

"Good idea. I'll take care of it. Talk to you later."

A few minutes later, he had his cousin on the line.

"Yes, I saw the article," Phil said.

"Surprised?"

"I would have been more surprised if your dad hadn't mentioned the possibility she was one of those Hathaways. But yes, I guess I *am* surprised because Claudia sure doesn't act like she's wealthy. I mean, she's really down-to-earth. Don't you think?"

"Yes, I do. Listen, do you want to go in with Jen and me and send some flowers?"

"I was thinking of sending some on my own."

"Oh, okay. But I thought you were cooling it with her. You know, giving her space." For a moment, John was irritated. Why did he keep having to remind Phil of what he'd decided? Why did Phil even *ask* for advice if he wasn't going to follow it? But John instantly realized he was being unfair, maybe even projecting his own frustration onto Phil's shoulders. After all, Phil had a perfect right to do whatever he wanted to do. John wasn't his keeper.

"Yeah, you're right," Phil said. "Maybe it *would* be better for the three of us to go together."

"Listen, if you want to send her flowers on your own, you go ahead and do it. Jen and I will send ours separately."

"No, you're right. We'll go together. What should we say on the card?"

"I don't know. How about just a simple 'with sympathy for your loss' kind of thing?"

After hanging up, John called and ordered the flowers. When he was finished, he looked at the clock. Only eight-thirty. Probably still too early to call Claudia. He'd wait till at least eleven, he decided, in case she was sleeping late.

He spent the morning looking at the footage of Travis Feeney they'd shot the day before. He was happy with what they had. It was almost noon before he had a chance to gain the privacy of his office and place the call to Claudia.

When Claudia's cell phone rang, she grabbed it out of her handbag. She was ready to switch it off and let her voice mail pick up a message when she saw the name and number on the caller ID screen

John!

With an apologetic glance at her mother, whom she and her sisters had been helping pick out a casket, Claudia rushed out of the funeral home's salesroom and into the more private hallway.

"Hello?" she said.

"Claudia? This is John. John Renzo."

Claudia couldn't help smiling. As if she wouldn't know who John was! "Hi, John."

"I heard about your father. I just wanted to say how sorry I am."

"Thank you."

"There was a nice article about him in the *Chronicle* this morning. Told all about your family."

So he knows… "Did it?"

"Yeah. Quite an impressive clan."

"John…I-I'm sorry I didn't tell you about them, but I just wanted to—"

"That's okay," he said, interrupting. "I think I understand why you didn't say anything."

"Do you?"

"I think so. I imagine you've had your share of people who wanted something from you as soon as they found out your background. In your shoes, I guess I'd be cautious, too."

Claudia drew a relieved breath. He *did* sound as if he understood. "I just didn't want you to think I didn't trust you or Jen…or Philip," she added belatedly.

"Hey, we have some family secrets, too."

His light tone lifted the last niggle of worry from her shoulders.

Voice serious again, he said, "Phil said you were planning to come back to work on Monday."

"Yes."

"In the meantime, do you want me to go over to your place and do anything? Pick up mail? Feed the cat?"

Claudia smiled. "I don't have a cat."

"What about the mail? I'll be happy to take care of it for you."

"I already asked the on-site manager to keep it for me, but thanks, John. I really appreciate your thoughtfulness and your friendship. Oh, and I'm sorry to miss your party Saturday."

"I've canceled it."

"You've *canceled* it? But…why?"

"I'd rather wait and have it when you and Sally can come."

"But—"

"I know. You won't be in the mood for a party any-time soon. That's okay. It's no big deal. Maybe I'll just wait and have something at Christmas."

He was so matter of fact, she couldn't say anything more without *making* a big deal out of his decision. And yet, *wasn't* it? Wasn't he telling her something he couldn't actually put into words? For the first time in the past two days, Claudia's sadness lifted.

"Well," he said, "I'm sure you're busy, so I'd bet-ter let you go. But if you think of *anything* I can do for you while you're gone, call me, okay?"

"Okay."

After that, there was an awkward pause. This was the time when, if they were involved, they would say something loving. Claudia wished she could. Oh, how she wished she could.

"Take care, Claudia. I'll be thinking of you."

And I'll be thinking of you. "Thank you, John. And thank you for calling. It means more than I can say."

Claudia didn't immediately return to the salesroom after she hung up. She just couldn't bring herself to leave the circle of warmth and comfort John's voice and his words had created around her for the cold, hard realities of death. She wanted to replay the phone call, think about what he'd said and the way he'd said it, and if that was selfish, well, maybe she deserved to be selfish once in a while.

"Claudia?"

Claudia's head jerked up. Lorna stood a few feet away.

"Is everything all right?"

Claudia nodded. "Yes, I, um, just had a phone call I needed to take."

"You're *sure* everything's okay?" Lorna's eyes were curious as she studied Claudia's face.

Claudia took a deep breath. "Yes. I'm sure. Is Mom finished?"

"Yeah. She finally settled on the bronze with the cream satin interior." Lorna made a face. "As if it matters," she muttered. She inclined her head toward two mauve velvet chairs across the hall. "Let's go sit down. They'll be out in a few minutes. She was just signing some forms."

Claudia put her phone back in her purse.

"So who was the call from?" Lorna said when they were seated.

Claudia smiled. "John."

"*The* John?"

"Yes. *The* John."

"Aha. Things have changed."

Claudia's smile faded. She shook her head. "Not really."

"But he *called* you…."

"Yes, but nothing's really different."

"So why'd he call?"

"Just to say he'd read about Dad in the morning paper and to offer to take care of anything that might need doing in Houston."

"That was nice."

"Yes, very nice."

"He sounds thoughtful and considerate."

"He is."

"You know, maybe I was wrong before. Maybe you *should* confront the situation. Just tell Philip how you feel and tell John, too. See what happens."

Claudia shook her head. "No, you were right. If anyone makes a move, it has to be John. Otherwise, even if we were to get together as a result, someday he might resent me, especially if our getting together resulted in an estrangement between him and Philip."

Lorna nodded, then sighed deeply. "Love isn't all it's cracked up to be, is it?"

The next few days would always be a blur in Claudia's mind. The incessant phone calls, the cards and flowers and plants arriving hourly at the house, the unexpected appearance of her mother's brother Paul—whom they rarely saw because he lived in Florida and was not close to Kathleen—and then the ordeal of the viewing at Resthaven.

Hundreds of people came. Claudia shook so many hands and fielded so many sympathetic wishes, she wondered if there was any person left within a hundred-mile radius who *wasn't* there at some point in the evening. She tried to tell herself this was a tribute to her father, that he'd mattered, but realistically she knew the main draw was curiosity about the Hathaways.

Then there was the funeral itself—a much more extravagant and pompous affair than Claudia would have preferred, but she hadn't been asked her opinion. All the arrangements had been made by her mother and approved by her grandmother. This, too, drew an enormous crowd.

Through everything, her grandmother was a marvel. She was gracious and kind to all the people who expressed their sympathy and she refused any special treatment except for the aid of her grandson, who gave her his arm in support.

After the funeral, she remained in her seat in the drawing room of the big house and keenly observed those who had been invited back to the house.

It was nearly seven before everyone left.

After her grandmother had gone off to bed and the servants—supervised by Kathleen—began the cleanup, Lorna said, "Why don't you come stay at my house tonight?"

"That would be wonderful," Claudia said gratefully. She'd been dreading the departure of Bryce and Amy and the children. Although she enjoyed her sister Chloe, now that her husband was there, she seemed preoccupied. And Claudia had no interest in listening to her Uncle Paul drone on and on about his insurance agency and how successful it was, which he'd been doing for hours to anyone who would listen. Why was it that people who were crashing bores never seemed to realize it? "But I'd better check with Mom first. Make sure she doesn't need me."

"No, you go ahead," her mother said. "As soon as the cleanup is finished, I'm going to bed."

"You're sure?"

"Claudia, I'm perfectly fine. Don't hover."

"I'll just be a minute," Claudia said to Lorna, then dashed upstairs to pack her things.

Ten minutes later, they were on their way.

Lorna built a fire in her fireplace, and the sisters put on their pajamas and curled up on the sofa with glasses of wine. The quiet was heavenly. After awhile, they began to talk. Both wondered what life would be like for their mother now. It wouldn't be easy with just her and their grandmother rattling around that huge house together.

"Don't let Gran pressure you into coming back here," Lorna said.

"Oh, don't worry. I won't." Even if it hadn't been for the fact Claudia loved her job in Houston, how could she bear to be so far away from John?

"She'll try, you know."

"I know. She's already tried, as a matter of fact."

Lorna turned her wineglass around thoughtfully. "Would it surprise you to know I've been thinking about moving away, too?"

Claudia almost choked on the wine she'd just swallowed. "You're not serious."

Lorna's gaze met hers. She nodded.

"But Lorna, you *love* your job. And Bryce. Ohmigod, you're like his right-hand person."

"I know."

Claudia stared at her sister. "You *are* serious."

Lorna sighed heavily. "Yes. Oh, I wouldn't do anything immediately. I'd wait a bit to let things settle down. But maybe in the spring…"

"What brought this on?"

Lorna shrugged. "I don't know. I just…" She looked down at her glass. "I want children so badly, and I'm not getting any younger."

"Oh, Lorna."

"There's just not much chance of me meeting anyone here." She looked up and smiled. "You figured that out, didn't you?"

Claudia nodded. Morgan Creek was too small a town. All the ambitious men Lorna's age had gone looking for greener pastures long ago. The ones who were left either had no ambition, weren't husband material, or were already married.

"Where would you go? Austin?"

"I'm not sure. I actually thought about Houston."

"Lorna! That would be wonderful. I'd love to have you come to Houston."

"Listen, don't say anything to anyone, okay? As I said, I wouldn't do anything before spring, especially since we're getting ready to launch our new doughnut sweetshops in January, but when I do decide something, I want to break it to Bryce first."

"Oh, I won't breathe a word."

After that, they finished their wine and headed off to bed. It took Claudia a long time to fall asleep. Her brain was on overload. Too much had happened in the past week and she hadn't yet had a chance to process it all.

Her last thought before succumbing to the exhaustion of the past few days was of John and how, in a perfect world, he'd be here with her.

The reading of Jonathan's will took place the next morning at the house. At ten o'clock, the family gathered in the drawing room. After Mrs. Janny and Lucy, one of the maids, had brought in the coffee and tea service, along with freshly baked Hathaway sweet rolls and scones, Luther Hirsch, who handled the family's personal business, stood and cleared his throat.

"Jonathan's will is fairly straightforward," he said. "Except for some special bequests, he has left his half ownership of this home and all other buildings on the estate to his wife, Kathleen. In addition, she automatically became the sole owner of their joint bank accounts and investments.

"His stock in the family business, worth approximately thirty million dollars in today's market, was—for tax purposes—long ago put into trusts for each of you children, with special trusts set up for each grandchild, as well.

"You'll each receive detailed instructions concerning your personal trust fund and what your options are. Generally speaking, each child owns about five million dollars worth of stock, with the remainder divided among the grandchildren."

Five million dollars.

Claudia was stunned.. Of course she'd known her family was wealthy, but she'd had no idea there was that much. No wonder people had treated her like some kind of celebrity when they'd met her.

I don't want it. I'm going to give it all away.

But even as she told herself this, she recalled what Sally had told her on the phone last night. After a major shock like this, a person shouldn't make any big decisions right away.

Such as giving away five million dollars. Or rushing back to Houston to tell John he was the only man whose comfort she would welcome.

Chapter Eleven

Claudia's first week back at work was exhausting. Although her classes had been covered while she was gone, she had a lot of catching up to do. Plus, after the world of Morgan Creek and the events surrounding her father's death, it took her awhile to switch gears and settle back into the groove of teaching and her life in Houston.

She'd been afraid Philip would use her father's death as an excuse to hover around her again, but he seemed to sense that would be a mistake, so except for offering her a sympathetic ear should she want to talk, he pretty much left her alone for the first part of the week.

By Thursday she began to think he had finally realized she wasn't interested in him and wasn't going to ask to see her over the weekend. But her hopes were short-lived because right after her last student left, he knocked on the frame of her door to get her attention, then walked into her classroom.

"Hi," he said, smiling.

"Hi." Oh, why couldn't she feel about him the way she felt about John? She remembered how Sally had said she was a fool. She guessed she was.

"How're you doing?" His eyes and voice were filled with concern.

Claudia sighed inwardly, wishing she could love him. His only fault was he wasn't John. "I'm doing okay."

He smiled again. "I brought you something." So saying, he put a small silver box on her desk.

"What's this?" Claudia picked up the box.

He shrugged. "Something I saw that made me think of you."

She didn't know what to say. Because she didn't, she opened the box. Inside, lying on a bed of cotton was a delicate silver bangle bracelet, set on one side with an aquamarine, her birthstone.

Even if the aquamarine was just a fake, and surely it *was,* Claudia wasn't sure she should keep the bracelet. Wouldn't that be sending the wrong message? Yet she didn't know how to refuse without causing hurt feelings and an awkwardness she wasn't sure she could deal with.

"What's wrong? Don't you like it?"

"Yes, it's lovely, but—"

"But what?"

"But I don't think I can accept it."

"Why not?"

He seemed genuinely perplexed.

"Because we're not..." Claudia sighed. "Look, it's not like we're a couple. I just don't feel comfortable taking this." Surely now he'd take the hint.

"It's just a bracelet, Claudia. And we *are* friends, aren't we?"

"Yes, but—"

"And friends occasionally give each other gifts, especially when they're going through a bad time." He smiled. "You're making more of this than it is. It's really not that big a deal."

She remembered how John had said it wasn't a big deal to cancel his party, and how much that had meant to her. But she loved John. And she didn't love Philip.

"Come on, put it on."

Because to continue to refuse seemed mean, she lifted the bracelet out of the box and slipped it over her hand to join the others she'd put on that morning. The translucent blue gem caught the light. "Thank you, but promise me you won't do something like this again."

"I promise. And Claudia, I was thinking…"

She braced herself for what she was sure was coming.

"How would you like to do something really different this weekend? I was thinking maybe we could go ice-skating Sunday afternoon."

"Ice-skating? I haven't ice-skated since I was a kid." Now why had she said that? Why hadn't she just said she was busy?

"I haven't either, but there's a new rink at Memorial City, and it looks like it would be fun."

"It probably *would* be, Philip, but after a week at home, I have so much catching up to do. I really planned to work the whole weekend."

"Ah, come on, Claudia, you need *some* downtime. And it would be good for you to do something fun, something that will take your mind off your father."

"I'm sure you're right, but I'm so behind, and I really need Sunday afternoon to get some things done around the house."

"It doesn't have to be the *whole* afternoon. Maybe just a couple of hours."

Bracelet or no bracelet, Claudia hardened her heart. "I appreciate the thought, but I just can't." She almost added *this weekend* and stopped herself just in time. *Don't give him any opening.*

He looked as if he were going to keep trying to change her mind, but then he just nodded and said,

"Okay. I won't push you." Then he smiled. "But next weekend, I'm not going to take 'no' for an answer."

After he left, she put her head in her hands. *I can't keep this up. When will he stop? When will he realize it will never work between us? What do I have to do? Hit him over the head? Say something ugly?*

Driving home, it was hard not to feel completely discouraged. She hadn't seen or heard from John since she'd been back, and that didn't help, either. The only contact had been a delivery of a flowering azalea plant on Monday with a card that simply said: *Welcome back. John.*

So impersonal, she thought. And yet, what else had she expected? A declaration of undying love? *You know that's not going to happen.*

She tried to shake off her gloomy mood, but it refused to be shaken. After she'd had dinner—a frozen macaroni-and-cheese entrée and a salad—and had taken care of the next day's lesson planning, she was trying to decide whether to watch television or go to bed and read, when Jennifer called.

"Saturday night there's going to be a reception and a private showing of the video John shot for the Fairchild Cancer Center," she said. "I thought you might like to go with me."

Claudia's spirits immediately perked up. *John.* "I'd love to. Where's it going to be held?"

"At a new hotel in the museum district. It's supposed to be gorgeous."

"So I should dress up?"

"I'd say yes. Oh, and they're also having a silent auction, and I understand they had some fabulous things donated. All the money raised will go toward the new children's play center at Fairchild."

"Sounds great. I'll bring my checkbook."

They made arrangements for Jennifer to pick Claudia up at seven, then Jennifer said, "Are you doing okay?"

"Yeah, I'm fine."

"I can't imagine what it must be like to lose your dad. I'd be crushed if something happened to mine."

Claudia nodded over the sudden lump in her throat. It was still hard for her to believe her father was gone.

"How's your mom doing?"

"She's okay. She's a strong woman. And the truth is, they didn't have a great marriage."

"Oh. I'm sorry."

"Nothing to be sorry about. It was very thoughtful of you to ask, and I appreciate it. You're a good friend."

"Thanks."

"So…you're starting your new job Monday, right?"

"Yes. I'm really excited, Claudia."

"I know just how you feel. Are they taking you out to lunch tomorrow or anything?"

"Riley is."

"Oh, yes, Riley. I almost forgot. So how's it going with him?"

"Oh, Claudia, things are so good I'm almost afraid to say it for fear of jinxing myself."

Claudia couldn't prevent the stab of envy. "He's that wonderful, huh?"

"He's perfect. We've been together half a dozen times since that night at my house, and each time has been better than the last."

"I'm happy for you. You deserve this."

"Thanks," Jennifer said softly. "Sometimes I have to pinch myself to make sure it's not a dream. I just never thought I'd find anyone I could care for as much as I cared for Matt."

"Sometimes things work out the way they're supposed to," Claudia said. *Or at least they do for some people.*

"Hi, Phil. Glad I caught you."

"Oh, hi, Jen."

"I just wondered if you were planning to go to the reception and advance showing of John's video tonight?"

"I wouldn't miss it."

"Do you want to ride with me and Claudia?"

Philip blinked. "Claudia's going?" Hadn't Claudia said she had to work all weekend?

"Uh-huh. I called her the other night to invite her."

No, she hadn't said *all* weekend. She'd said she had to work on Sunday. "Well, hey, that'd be great. But why don't I drive and pick you two up instead?"

"Oh, I don't mind driving. We'll swing by to get you about seven-fifteen, okay?"

"Look, Jen, if I drive, I can take Claudia home last."

She was silent for a few seconds. "I don't know. I don't feel right about that. I mean, if you wanted to take Claudia to the reception, why didn't you ask her?"

"If I had, she would have refused. C'mon, Jen, help me out here. It's not a big deal who drives, is it?"

"I'm sorry, Phil. Maybe you should just drive yourself. Then, if you want to, you can ask to take Claudia home."

Realizing he wasn't going to win, he finally said, "No, that's okay. I shouldn't have tried to put you in the middle. I know you're Claudia's friend."

"Yes, I am, but I'm *your* cousin and I love you. Still, it would be wrong of me to try to make Claudia do something she doesn't want to do. You do understand, don't you?"

"Yeah, I do. Don't worry. It's fine. I appreciate you asking me, and I'll be ready when you get here."

Claudia tried on ten different outfits before deciding on a short violet crepe dress with a slit up the back. She paired it with strappy black suede Jimmy Choo sandals and long, glittery amethyst earrings.

After grabbing her long black velvet coat from her closet, she hurried downstairs. She'd taken so long to get ready, she was afraid Jennifer might already be waiting out front. But Claudia had timed it just right. Jennifer pulled up just as Claudia emerged from her front door.

"That's a gorgeous coat," Jennifer said.

"Thanks. I rarely get to wear it." Claudia fastened her seat belt as Jennifer pulled away from the curb.

"It's fun to get dressed up once in a while, isn't it?"

Claudia nodded happily. She was excited about tonight. She wondered if Philip would be there. She hoped not. It would be so much more fun for her if she didn't have to worry about him dogging her the entire night. But at least she was with Jennifer, so even if he was there, she wouldn't have to worry about him wanting to bring her home.

"I hope you don't mind, but we're picking Philip up."

Claudia almost said *oh, no* but caught herself in time. "No, that's fine." Inwardly, she was cringing. Why couldn't she ever seem to get away from him?

And yet, why was she surprised? After all, Jennifer *was* Philip's cousin, and Claudia knew how close they were. Jennifer probably thought she was doing Claudia a favor by including Philip in their plans.

You should have told Jennifer how you feel about Philip. Then she'd understand, and she wouldn't keep trying to throw the two of you together.

"Are you *sure* you don't mind?"

Claudia shook off her thoughts. "No, of course not."

"Oh, good. I was a little worried after I asked him. I mean, I know you two have been dating."

Have been dating. They'd been out together a sum total of three times.

"He really likes you, Claudia," Jennifer said softly.

"I know."

"And you…?" The question hung in the air.

"He's a really nice guy, but—"

"But?"

Claudia took a deep breath. "But that's all."

"Oh."

"This isn't going to make things awkward between you and me, is it?"

"Of course not! I mean, I wish you felt about Philip the way he feels about you, but your relationship with him has nothing to do with *our* relationship."

Relief flooded Claudia. Maybe things really *would* be all right. *Yeah, but she doesn't know about John, now does she?*

"Besides," Jennifer was saying, "who knows? Sometimes friendships turn into something more. Like you said, Phil is a really nice guy."

Claudia decided to let the statement stand unanswered and Jennifer dropped the subject.

By then they were nearly to his townhouse, anyway, because it turned out to be only a mile or so from where Claudia lived. It was the first time she'd seen his place, which was located in a small complex on a quiet street.

He must have been watching for them because Jennifer had no sooner pulled her car into the drive than he came outside.

"Maybe I should sit in back," Claudia said.

"Don't be silly. He can get in the back."

"But his legs are longer, and there's more room up here."

"Claudia, he'll be fine." Jennifer reached over and squeezed Claudia's arm. "Relax."

They both turned to say hello when he opened the back door and climbed in. He grinned. "How'd I get so lucky? The two prettiest girls in Houston, and I get to be with them."

"Flatterer," Jennifer said with a laugh.

Claudia didn't comment. She felt extremely uncomfortable and wished Jennifer had told her ahead of time she was going to ask Philip to come with them instead of just doing it and asking if she minded afterward. *Would you have been any* more *prepared if you'd known?*

"I'm glad you're going tonight, Claudia," Philip said, leaning forward and giving her a smile.

"Thank you. I'm looking forward to it."

"John's a little nervous," Jennifer said. "A lot is riding on this project."

"He doesn't need to worry," Philip said, "he does great work."

"You know that, and I know that, and most of time,

he knows that, too, but still…there will be a lot of influential people there tonight, so it *is* a little nerve-racking for him."

It didn't take them long to reach the hotel.

The ballroom where the viewing and reception were being held turned out to be on the top floor, fifteen stories up. When they walked in, the first thing Claudia saw was the breathtaking view of the downtown skyline from a wall-long expanse of window. "Wow," she said. "This is beautiful."

"Sure is," Jennifer agreed.

Claudia and Jennifer checked their coats, then the three of them walked slowly through the crowd looking for John. They found him standing by the bar, surrounded by several people, including two very attractive women, one of whom was hanging on his arm and looking at him as if he were the most fascinating man in the room.

Claudia instantly hated her.

His face lit up when he saw them. For just a moment, his eyes met Claudia's and something flickered in their depths. Just that one look was enough to hollow out Claudia's stomach. She was intensely aware of Philip beside her, and when he put his hand on the small of her back in a proprietary gesture, it was all she could do to keep from wrenching away. *I don't belong to you! Why can't you see that?*

John walked over to meet them and Claudia subtly

shifted position so that Philip was no longer touching her. She was glad to see the woman who had been clinging to John had finally let him go, but she was still watching him.

"Hey," John said. "Glad you guys made it." He kissed Jennifer's cheek, shook Philip's hand, then turned to Claudia. Smiling, he leaned over and kissed her cheek, too. "How're you doing, Claudia?"

Claudia wasn't sure how she managed, but she kept her cool, smiled and said, "I'm fine."

"When did you get back?"

"Monday." Just these few words exchanged had made her heart pick up speed.

"Well, we missed you."

"Thank you."

"When's the video going to be shown?" Philip asked.

"At eight-thirty."

Claudia looked at her watch. It was seven forty-five.

"There's food down at the other end," John said. "And, of course, the bar."

"Want something to eat?" Jennifer asked Claudia.

"I'm not really hungry."

"Me either."

"But I'd love a glass of wine."

"I'll get one for you," John said. "White or red?"

"Red for me," Claudia said.

"And red for me," Jennifer said.

Philip went with John, and Claudia welcomed the respite. Although she'd been in situations before when both men were present, for some reason, she felt nervous tonight.

"You okay?" Jennifer said.

"Yeah, I'm fine. Why?"

"You just seem tense. It's because of Phil, isn't it?"

Claudia figured it was useless to deny it. "It *is* a bit awkward."

"I'm sorry. I won't do this to you again."

But if Jennifer stopped inviting her places where Philip might be, that meant Claudia would never get to see John. This might be the last time she'd be in his company unless they should accidentally meet.

When it was time for the showing of the video, all the guests were ushered into a smaller room where chairs had been set up theater-style. She and Jen found two seats together, and Claudia was relieved that Philip ended up sitting with John. Now she could enjoy the video.

Claudia was thrilled for John. The video was fantastic: moving, absorbing and inspirational all at once. After it was over, she would have liked to congratulate him, but he was once more surrounded by people, so she decided it would have to wait until later.

But she never got the chance. For the rest of the evening, the Fairchild people seemed to have commandeered him. Even Jen said she didn't feel comfortable approaching him when he was busy with clients.

Suddenly Claudia wished she hadn't come. Not seeing John at all was preferable to being near him, yet not with him.

The situation was more hopeless than ever and the sooner she accepted that, the better for everyone.

John had just poured his morning coffee when his cell phone rang. The caller ID showed Philip's number. "Hey, cuz, what's up?"

"Can I come over and talk to you?"

"Now?" It was only nine-thirty.

"Yeah, now."

"Is something wrong?"

"I'll tell you when I see you."

"Okay, sure, come on over. But give me twenty minutes, okay? I want to take a shower before you get here."

Twenty minutes later, on the dot, Phil was at the gate, buzzing for admittance. Moments later, John opened the door to let him in.

"I need your help," Philip said without preamble.

"Okay." John was thoroughly confused. He couldn't imagine what it was that was so important Phil had to come over early on a Sunday morning. Especially since he'd seen him last night and everything seemed to be fine. "Want some coffee?"

Philip nodded. "Yeah, sounds good."

Once they had their coffee, John said, "Okay, what is it? What's wrong?"

"It's Claudia."

John's heart sank. *I should have known.* "What about her?" he said cautiously.

"Nothing's working. I can't seem to get anywhere with her." Phil's eyes were bleak. "No matter what I do, it's wrong."

"What happened now?"

"Well, I bought her this bracelet and she didn't want to take—"

"Wait a minute. You bought her a *bracelet?* Why?"

"Because I saw it and it reminded me of her."

"You just happened to be looking at jewelry and you saw a bracelet that reminded you of her?"

"You don't have to sound so skeptical."

"Hell, Phil, I *am* skeptical. I mean, I wouldn't be caught dead looking at jewelry unless I was shopping for a gift for someone."

Phil had the grace to hang his head.

"Why'd you *do* that? I thought you were going to cool it with her. Give her some time."

Phil finally met John's eyes. "I just wanted to do something nice for her."

"So what happened?"

"She didn't want to take it, but I insisted."

John smothered a sigh. Why was Phil so damned dense sometimes? Jeez, didn't he know *anything* about women? "So what else happened?"

Phil shrugged. "No matter what I invite her to do,

she has a reason why she can't do it. On Thursday, I asked her to go ice-skating with me—just like you suggested—and she said she had too much work to do this weekend after being away last week. I didn't want to pressure her, so I said okay, I understood. Then she came to the reception last night. If she was so busy, why'd she have time to do that?"

"I thought you came together."

"No, we didn't," he said glumly. "Jennifer invited her, then she called me and suggested we all ride together."

"Oh." John drank some of his coffee.

"Will you talk to her for me, John?"

John nearly choked on his coffee. "What?"

"You know, plead my case for me?"

"But Phil, *you're* the one who should be doing that, not me."

"You're so much better at stuff like this. You know you are. Besides, I can't say what a great guy I am, but *you* can."

Jesus. How had he gotten himself into this? "Of course you can say you're a great guy. In fact, that's exactly what you *should* say. You should just tell her, flat out, how you feel about her and ask her to take a chance on you. Then tell her why she should."

Phil's shoulders slumped. He shook his head. "I can't."

"Phil…"

"Please, John. I'm feeling kind of desperate."

Oh, hell. He *did* owe Phil, more than he could ever repay. John heaved a sigh. "All right. I'll talk to her." But even as he promised, he couldn't help feeling impatient with Phil. One of these days he needed to stand on his own two feet.

"I knew you'd come through for me." Phil put his arm around John's shoulders. "I'll never forget this."

After promising Phil he'd talk to Claudia today and call him immediately afterward with a report, John sent Phil on his way. After Phil left, John moaned. "What the *hell* have I gotten myself into?" he muttered.

The last thing on earth he wanted to do was plead Phil's case for him. And yet, that's exactly what he was going to do.

Deciding that it was best to get the job over with as quickly as possible—before he lost his nerve—John picked up his cell phone.

When Claudia's phone rang a little after eleven on Sunday, she thought it was Lorna calling.

Her heart leaped when she saw John's number on the caller ID. Her hands trembled as she punched the On button. "Hello?"

"Claudia? Hi. This is John."

Claudia smiled. Her heart was beating like a tom-tom. "Hi, John."

"I didn't get you in the middle of anything, did I?"

"No. I just got home from church."

"Uh, I was wondering. Would it be okay if I came by? There's something I want to talk to you about."

Claudia could hardly breathe. "You mean now?"

"In about an hour. Unless you've got something planned?"

"Um, no. I, uh, planned to stay home today."

"So it'd be okay, then?"

"Sure. Um, do you know where I live?"

"I'm sure I can find it. You're on Potomac, right?"

"Yes." She gave him the number and explained which unit she lived in.

"Okay. I'll be there about noon."

Claudia just sat there after disconnecting the call. She couldn't believe she hadn't imagined the call. John was coming over! He wanted to talk to her. What could this mean? She was afraid to hope, and yet…

He must be coming to talk to her about their situation. What else could it *be?* She swallowed hard. *Oh, please God, please, please, please…*

She raced upstairs. She had just changed from her church outfit into old jeans and an oversized T-shirt because she'd planned to do some cleaning, but she sure as heck didn't want John to see her dressed like this. Especially if he was coming to tell her how he felt about her.

And that *must* be why he was coming.

It must be.

Claudia was so nervous, it was hard to think. What should she wear? She rooted through the clothes in her closet, finally settling on a pair of khaki carpenter pants and a wine-colored sweater.

Once she was dressed, she redid her makeup and fixed her hair again. Then she spritzed the air with her favorite perfume and walked through the mist—a trick she'd recently read about in a magazine.

Downstairs again, she poured herself a Coke. She needed something to settle her stomach, which felt as if a million butterflies were dancing in there. Taking deep breaths to calm herself, she sat at the kitchen table and sipped at her drink. Outside she could hear cars passing by, and from somewhere in the complex the faint strains of a violin concerto. Inside her kitchen, the clock on the wall ticked loudly, the refrigerator hummed and her heart beat far too quickly.

The minutes seemed to crawl by, but finally it was noon. Less than two minutes later, her doorbell rang.

She got up and walked slowly down the hall. In the narrow glass panel on the right side of her door, she saw John's shadowy outline.

Here goes everything, she thought, and opened the door.

Chapter Twelve

She was so beautiful.

John had rehearsed what he would say to Claudia ever since Phil had left him early this morning, but seeing her standing there, John realized that no matter how many times he'd told himself he could do this, he wasn't sure he could.

And yet he must.

No matter how stupid you think this mission is, no matter how much you wish you were here to tell her how you really feel, you owe Phil your best shot.

"Hi, John. Come on in," she said. Her smile said she was happy to see him.

"Hi." *Her whom I may not love...* Those words from

Longfellow's poem had haunted him…*taunted* him… ever since the day he'd called Claudia after her father's death. *Ever since the day I realized I loved her.* How was it possible to fall so deeply in love with a person when you hadn't spent much time with her at all?

"I just poured myself a Coke. Would you like something?"

"A Coke sounds good."

"Why don't you come into the kitchen with me while I get it?"

As he followed her down the short hallway, he wondered what she was thinking. Did she have any idea why he wanted to talk to her today? "This is a nice place you've got here."

"Thank you. I love it."

Her kitchen looked like her—fresh, bright, shining, with cheery yellow walls and blue accents. Centered on the oval walnut kitchen table sat a blue watering can filled with daisies. John thought of his own unadorned apartment kitchen.

Claudia opened the refrigerator and took out a two-liter bottle of Coke. Filling a glass with ice, she poured it three-quarters full.

"Do you want to sit in the living room? It's more comfortable there."

"Sure." The moment he agreed, he thought it would have been better to sit there, with the kitchen table between them. That would have been easier in a way he couldn't define.

Again, he followed her. When they walked into the living room, which was filled with sunlight, he realized that even if he hadn't known Claudia came from money, the room would have conveyed a subtle message of class and taste. Her furniture, in soft shades of gray, gold, green and blue, was a mixture of contemporary and traditional. Like its owner, John thought.

She sat on one of the buttery leather chairs flanking the fireplace and indicated he should take the other. Once he was seated, she looked at him expectantly.

"I hardly know where to begin," he said.

"Just begin." Her smile was encouraging.

Once more, he wondered what she was thinking. She didn't seem apprehensive. She seemed…buoyant, which made him hesitate. Damn, he didn't want to do this. He wished he'd tried to dissuade Phil a little harder. *Just get it over with.* "Phil came to see me this morning."

Her smile slowly faded. "Is something wrong? Has something happened?"

"No, no, nothing like that."

"That's good."

"I'm sorry if I alarmed you. I told you I didn't know where to begin."

Claudia frowned. She couldn't imagine why he seemed so reluctant. Almost afraid. Which wasn't like John at all. "John, just say it. Whatever it is, just tell me." Maybe he'd told Philip that he loved her. Could that be it? She took another deep breath. She couldn't seem to get her stomach to settle down.

"You'll probably tell me to butt out, that this is none of my business, but Phil's my cousin, and I…" He leaned forward, an expression in his dark eyes that she couldn't read. "The thing is, Phil's crazy about you, Claudia. And he's frustrated because he can't seem to get to first base. He asked me if I could help."

For a long moment, she just looked at him. "You came here to plead his case."

He nodded. "Yes. I told him he should come himself, but he seems to think he's done something wrong. Anyway, I just wanted to say that Phil's a great guy."

Disappointment had settled like a stone in her chest. "John, I'm sorry, but he wants something from me that I'm not capable of giving." *Not to him.*

"You don't think if you just gave him a chance, you might not change your mind?"

She shook her head. *Was I completely wrong about John? Have I only imagined he really cares for me? How can he say all these things about Philip if he has feelings for me himself?* "I won't change my mind. I'm never going to feel about him the way he wants me to. I've tried to let him down gently, but he just won't take the hint."

Outside, a dog barked and a car backfired. Life progressing normally. How could that be, she wondered, when her life was in such turmoil?

"So there's no hope at all? Nothing I can say that would make a difference?"

"No." She couldn't tear her gaze away. She *couldn't* have been wrong about John. Every signal he'd sent had told her he shared her feelings. And yet she knew he would never make the first move. *This is your chance. There may never be another.* From somewhere she dredged up the courage to say what needed saying. "The truth is, I'm in love with someone else." After the words were spoken, she felt as if a huge weight had been lifted from her shoulders. The dye was cast now, for better or worse.

John just looked at her. "Do you want me to tell him that?"

But Claudia's reserves of strength had been used up. And suddenly she knew she couldn't keep sitting there talking to him as if nothing important had happened here today. If he didn't leave soon, she was going to break down in front of him, and she'd rather die than do that. The stark reality was, if John didn't love her, he didn't love her. There was nothing she could do about it, just as there was nothing Philip could do about her lack of feelings for him. She stood. "I really don't care what you tell him. Now, if you don't mind, I think you should go."

He jumped to his feet. "I—I shouldn't have come."

"No, you shouldn't have." *Go. Just go.* She could

feel the tears welling. *Oh, God, please make him go.* She couldn't meet his gaze.

"Claudia, I—"

"Goodbye, John." Blindly, she walked toward the front door. Any moment, she knew she was going to fall apart. With all her strength, she tried to hold on to her emotions.

"Claudia…" He touched her shoulder.

She opened the door. Looked away. "Please, John. Please go."

"Claudia…" His voice sounded husky.

All of Claudia's defenses suddenly evaporated. The tears she'd successfully held back spilled over. Furious with herself, she brushed them away.

Gently, he lifted her chin and their eyes met. Through her tears, she saw the desperation on his face and knew it was a mirror of her own.

He kicked the door shut with his foot.

Later, she wouldn't have been able to say who made the first move. All she knew was, in the next moment, she was in his arms.

When his mouth met hers, she wrapped her arms around him and kissed him with all the pent-up need she'd suppressed for so long. The kiss went on and on. Became two kisses. Then three.

Soon kisses weren't enough. He pushed his hands up under her sweater and cupped her breasts. Claudia moaned as his thumbs touched her nipples. In seconds, he had removed her sweater and was unhooking her bra. Soon they were tearing each other's clothes off. It was as if, waiting this long for one another, they couldn't wait another second.

There was no tenderness.

No finesse.

There were only arms and legs, hungry mouths and hands, heated skin against heated skin. John pushed her up against the wall. As his mouth devoured hers, he ground against her.

Claudia was past reason. There was nothing in her universe but this urgency, this wanting, this fire inside her. She dug her nails into his back. She could feel his erection straining against her, wanting access.

"Now," she cried, "now!"

He lifted her up and plunged into her.

The feel of him, the steel and heat of him, demolished her last bit of control, and she wound her legs around him and buried her face in his neck.

Grunting, he continued to thrust, each time driving harder and deeper until Claudia could hold back no longer, and she fell apart around him in a shattering climax. A second later, with a loud cry, he shuddered with his own release.

For a long moment, they held each other as their bodies and their breathing calmed. Then slowly, he released her. When he didn't say anything, wouldn't even *look* at her, fear wormed its way into her heart.

Finally she could stand the silence no longer. "John?" she whispered.

He took a long, ragged breath

"John?" she said again.

Finally he met her eyes. "I'm sorry. This was wrong. It should never have happened."

Claudia froze. Sorry? He was *sorry?* She bit down on her lip to keep it from trembling.

"I—I have to go."

Claudia's first instinct was to grab hold of him, to make him look at her, really *look* at her. But pride wouldn't allow her to beg. So she bent down, gathered up her clothes and walked to the steps. She didn't turn around. "Please close the door on your way out." And then she began to climb.

John hated himself.

What had he *done?*

And how was he going to face Phil?

If Phil ever found out what had happened today, he'd never forgive John.

And Claudia… John wasn't sure he'd ever forget the look on Claudia's face when he left her.

Please close the door on your way out.

He'd never forget the finality of those words. She hated him now, too. And he didn't blame her.

John drove home blindly.

What should he do? *Maybe I should move back to*

Austin. His old company would take him back in a minute. But how would he explain such a move to his family? They would think he was crazy.

Better to be thought crazy than to be thought a Judas. John could just imagine what Jen would think, what she would *say,* if she ever found out about his behavior today. Bad enough that he'd betrayed Phil, but then he'd treated Claudia as if she were nothing to him.

But what else could he have done? He couldn't say he loved her. If he had, he wouldn't have been able to go. And he *had* to go. Because staying wasn't an option.

Now his best hope was that someday she'd find it in her heart to forgive him.

"Did you talk to her?"

"Yes, I talked to her."

"And?"

John wished he could just crawl into a hole. "I'm sorry, Phil. She said she hopes the two of you can always be friends, but that's it."

"Nothing else?"

John shook his head. "No, nothing else."

"But *why?* Did she say *why?*"

"Hell, Phil, it's not something that can be explained. You should know that. Jeez, Sarah's been sending out signals for at least a year, and you're not interested. I mean, come on. Sometimes interest is one-sided."

"What do you mean, Sarah's been sending out signals?"

"Just what I said." John knew he shouldn't have said anything about Sarah, but sometimes Phil drove him crazy. *Don't blame* him *because you feel guilty.*

"*Sarah's* interested in me?"

John bit back a smart-ass answer. "Look, I'm sorry. I did my best." *I've turned into a world-class liar.*

"I know you did. And I appreciate it. So you think it's hopeless?"

"Yes, it's hopeless. Time to move on."

And it's time for me to move on, too.

Somehow Claudia got through the week. She had dreaded seeing Philip, but he simply said *hello* when he saw her in the halls and didn't stop. That was fine with her. She really didn't care what he thought. All she wanted was to be left alone.

Every night she cried herself to sleep. At first, she'd thought surely John would call. Say he hadn't meant what he'd said. That he wasn't sorry. That the only thing he was sorry about was doing something behind his cousin's back, but that now he intended to put things right. She'd envisioned him confronting Philip and telling him the truth, then coming back to her.

But John didn't call.

And as the week approached its end, she knew he wasn't going to.

Friday morning she packed some clothes and as soon as her last class was over, she headed straight for Morgan Creek.

Everything was ruined now, she knew. She wasn't even sure her friendship with Jennifer would survive because being friends with Jennifer would mean being thrown into John's company from time to time, and Claudia couldn't handle that. It had been bad enough before, but now it would be impossible.

As she drove, she berated herself for being so stupid because what had happened between her and John had been her fault. If she hadn't forced the issue, he would have left her the same way he found her—a woman who could never be anything more than his friend.

You deserve to be miserable.

But down deep, she knew that wasn't true. No one deserved to be miserable. And what had she said or done that was so terrible? She'd just told the truth—a truth both she and John were trying to pretend didn't exist.

By the time she reached Morgan Creek, she was exhausted from thinking and beating up on herself and thinking some more. The problem was, no matter how much she went over things in her mind, nothing would change.

She had made love with John.

And he had left her.

All she needed now was to find out she was pregnant. For that was the other stupid thing she'd done. She'd had sex without protection. The fact that it had happened unexpectedly was no excuse. She was a grown-up. She was supposed to think about consequences before she acted, not afterwards.

Of course, she hadn't been thinking at all last Sunday.

But that was going to change. She would never again do anything so foolish or so potentially dangerous.

Starting today.

As she pulled into the front turnaround of her family's home, she vowed that at least for this weekend, she would also stop thinking about John and stop lamenting what was done.

It was time to move forward.

"Claudia, is something wrong?"

Claudia looked at Lorna and shook her head. "No. Why do you ask?" It was Sunday morning. They had just come from having Sunday dinner with the family and were now sitting on Lorna's porch swing. Claudia planned to leave for Houston soon.

"You've seemed kind of down all weekend."

Claudia shrugged. "I'm fine. Truth is, I was wondering if *you* were feeling down."

"Me? Why?"

"Because of Amy's announcement." At dinner, Bryce's wife had told them she was pregnant and expecting a baby in the spring.

"Oh," Lorna said. "No, I'm happy for Bryce and Amy. It will be wonderful for them to have a child together. You know, it'll really cement their two families." She sighed. "I am envious, though."

Claudia nodded. She was, too. She'd looked at Amy's shining face and Bryce's proud smile and she'd felt such an ache of longing it had brought tears to her eyes.

After that, her vow not to think about John was useless, for his image refused to leave her mind.

She wished she could stay angry with him.

But she couldn't. The bottom line was, no matter what he'd done or not done, she loved him. And really, could she fault him? He'd yielded to a need as strong as hers, but he was an honorable man, and he'd felt he'd betrayed Philip by doing so.

Yet it hurt so much to know there would never be another time for them. Claudia sighed deeply. "I'd better be going. It's a long drive back, and I don't like traveling after dark."

"Okay."

The sisters hugged goodbye, with Lorna promising to come and visit soon, and then Claudia took off.

As she had on the drive in to Morgan Creek, she thought about John and their situation all the way home.

By the time she reached her condo, she had made a decision.

In the spring, she would look for another job, this time in either Dallas or Austin.

That would be best for everyone.

Chapter Thirteen

"I wish I knew what was wrong with Claudia."

John looked at his sister. It was the Tuesday before Thanksgiving and they were having lunch at a favorite Vietnamese restaurant near Jen's work. "Why? What's happened?"

"That's just it. I don't have any idea."

John knew he had to be careful, but it was so seldom he heard Claudia's name, and he was hungry for news of her. "What makes you think something is wrong?"

Jen twirled some Singapore curry noodles onto her fork. "She just doesn't seem herself."

"Do you see much of her?"

"No. That's the other thing. She's gone home every

weekend the past month, which really limits the time we can spend together. We've met for dinner a couple of times during the week and talked on the phone, but that's it."

"Don't you think it's normal that she's going home so often? I mean, it's only been about six weeks or so since her father died."

"That's true."

But she didn't sound convinced, and secretly, John wondered, too, if that were the only reason Claudia was leaving town every weekend. *Oh, don't be an ass. Just because you can't get* her *out of* your *mind doesn't mean she feels the same way. Maybe she thinks good riddance.*

"I don't know," Jen continued. "I could be all wrong, but I think there's something other than her father's death that's bothering her." She took another bite. "I wonder if Phil's talked to her."

"Phil?"

"Well, they *do* work together." She frowned. "*What?* Why do you look like that?"

"Phil didn't tell you what happened, did he?" John had been sure he would.

"No." She blotted her mouth with her napkin. "What's going on, John? Obviously, *something's* happened that you're not telling me."

"It wasn't my place to say anything." John sighed. "Oh, hell." Then he launched into the safe version of his visit to Claudia.

Jen listened quietly.

"I knew she wasn't interested in him," she said when he'd finished.

"How? Female intuition? Or did she tell you?"

"She told me."

John wondered what else Claudia had told Jen. Had she mentioned *him?* He'd have given anything to ask. "When was this?"

"The night we went to the Fairchild reception."

John thought about how gorgeous Claudia had looked that night. And how frustrated he'd been because she was there, but she wasn't with him, and there wasn't a damned thing he could do about it, just like there wasn't a damned thing he could do about the present situation. "I guess she's going home for Thanksgiving," he said.

"I'm sure she is."

John couldn't help thinking how, if they were a couple, he would probably be going with her. He wondered what her home was like. Her family. What would they think of him? Would they think he was good enough for her? Or would they think he was after her money?

With painful clarity, he realized he would never know these things. Claudia and everything and everyone that made up her life was lost to him forever.

Claudia no longer cried herself to sleep at night. The ache was still there, but now it was muted, hidden, the way an intermittent toothache was hidden.

Every once in a while, it would show its face, and then she'd keenly feel the loss of John. But for the most part, she was doing better. Not good, just better.

She knew her decision to leave Houston at the end of the school year had made the difference. Now she had something hopeful to cling to. A time when she wouldn't constantly be reminded of John or be tempted to call him.

It was so hard to avoid being with Jen too much, and that was another loss. Claudia knew if she spent too much time with Jen, she was liable to say something she shouldn't, and the last thing she wanted was for Jen to know about the episode with John.

She began marking the days off her calendar. One hundred eighty-two days and then she could escape. It bothered her to realize she would be running away, but realistically, what other choice did she have?

The Monday after Thanksgiving, John was given a new assignment, this one in Galveston for one of the luxury home builders who wanted a classy promotional video to send to prospective customers.

By Wednesday, he and his crew were there working. They hoped to have all the footage shot by Saturday at the latest. Although this wasn't a prestigious or challenging job, John was glad to have it. Glad to be out of Houston and everything there that reminded him of Claudia.

Sometimes he wasn't sure he'd ever get over her.

* * *

The weekend after Thanksgiving, Claudia stayed in Houston. She had to. She was so behind on laundry, cleaning, shopping and general errands, staying put one weekend was a necessity.

After her Friday classes, she stopped at her neighborhood Randall's before going home. She was in the produce department, picking out tomatoes, when she spied a man at the other end near the fruit. His back was to her, but she knew it was John. Same dark tousled hair, same black leather jacket, same black jeans.

Her heart began to pound. Blindly putting the selected tomatoes in her basket, she wondered what she should do. She wasn't sure she could talk to him without making a fool of herself. Yet her heart yearned toward him.

For the truth was, she was no longer angry with him or even disappointed. She knew he'd done what he had to do when he left her. And she badly wanted to tell him she understood. So she took a deep breath, told herself she could do this, and began to push her basket in his direction.

She was only a few feet away when he turned around.

He wasn't John.

Her disappointment was so acute, she felt it as a physical blow. Blinking back tears, she finished her shopping and drove home.

For the rest of the evening—while she fixed herself a bacon, lettuce and tomato sandwich, while she ate, while she cleaned the bathroom—she thought about John and how much she needed to tell him how she felt.

At midnight, she got out of bed, turned on her computer and composed an e-mail to send to him.

Dear John,

I've wanted to call you so many times since that day at my house. But for a long time I was too hurt, and after that I wasn't sure what to say or how you would react.

But I can't let things go the way we left them. I want you to know that nothing that happened between us was your fault, and I don't want you to blame yourself for it. I also want you to know I will never be sorry we made love. I am only sorry you feel so guilty about it, because I know you do. I know that's why you couldn't look at me and why you said what you did.

But John, you've taken nothing away from Philip, because I was never his and I never will be. So please stop blaming yourself. I wanted you to make love to me. I've wanted that for a long time.

She almost said she still wanted it, then thought better of it.

She signed off by saying she would always wish him well and hoped he felt the same way about her.

I'm trying to avoid spending a lot of time with Jen because I think it would be too awkward if you and I should happen to be thrown together, but that doesn't mean I harbor any bad feelings toward you. Please don't ever think that.

She paused. She didn't know how to sign the e-mail. Finally she just wrote I hope your career continues to go well, and I'll always wish you only the best. I'll never forget you.

Then, figuring what the heck, she signed it With love, Claudia.

Before she could lose her nerve, she pressed Send.

"Dammit!"

"What's wrong, John?" This came from Brigitte, the PA.

"I left a file at home. And I need it. It's the one with the script." John couldn't believe it. He went through everything in the project folder, and the file simply wasn't there. How could he have forgotten it? And now what? If he drove back to Houston to get it, they wouldn't finish the job today and would have to come back on Monday.

"Why don't you call Blackburn?" Blackburn was their client contact on the project.

"Because he told me he was going to Louisiana for the weekend." John thought hard. Maybe he could get

Jen or Phil to go over to the apartment and find the file, then attach it to an e-mail and send it to the hotel.

He decided he would call Jen first, and if he couldn't reach her, he'd call Phil. Ever since the day he'd gone to Claudia's to talk to her on Phil's behalf, John had been—if not avoiding Phil—at least not seeking out his company. The problem was, there had never been secrets between them. Their relationship wasn't perfect. John got impatient and irritated with Phil, and he knew Phil sometimes resented him and his greater confidence, but at heart, they loved each other and they were honest with each other.

So keeping this huge secret from Phil had made John uncomfortable in his cousin's presence.

But Jen wasn't home, and she didn't answer her cell phone, either. So John had no choice. He called Phil.

"Sure, I'll go," Phil said.

"You're sure you don't mind?"

"No, I don't mind. Besides, it'll only take what? Thirty minutes or so? An hour, tops."

"Thanks. You're saving my life. Again."

Phil laughed. "That means I own you, right? Isn't that what the Chinese say?"

"I think they say you're responsible for me."

"I'd rather own you."

Phil let himself into John's apartment and headed for the bedroom. After booting up John's computer, he searched for the file John wanted and found it. Then he switched over to John's e-mail program.

When he opened the program, it began downloading new e-mail. Phil leaned back and idly watched it. Suddenly he sat up. The last e-mail message to download was from Claudia.

Claudia!

What was she doing e-mailing John?

Phil knew it was wrong, but he couldn't help himself. He opened the e-mail.

As he read, his heart hammered.

I also want you to know I will never be sorry we made love.

They'd made love!

I am only sorry you feel so guilty about it, because I know you do. I know that's why you couldn't look at me and why you said what you did.

But John, you've taken nothing away from Philip, because I was never his and I never will be. So please stop blaming yourself. I wanted you to make love to me. I've wanted that for a long time.

Philip was shaking by the time he finished reading. He was so hurt and so angry, all he wanted to do was race down to Galveston and confront John. Although Philip had never been a violent man, he knew in his present state of mind he could beat John into a bloody pulp.

He couldn't believe John had betrayed him like this. And then he'd had the nerve to come and see him and pretend he'd tried his best with Claudia.

He'd tried his best all right! He'd tried his best for *himself.*

Philip sat there for a long time. He reread Claudia's e-mail, then read it again. The last time he read it, he really thought about what she was saying.

You've taken nothing away from Philip, because I was never his and I never will be. So please stop blaming yourself.

Philip sighed deeply. Then he closed her post and created a new e-mail. This one he addressed to the hotel where John was staying and attached the file John needed. Once the message and attachment were sent, he reopened Claudia's e-mail to John and printed off a copy.

Then he shut the e-mail program down and turned off John's computer.

An hour later he was on his way to Galveston.

John waited at the hotel until his file came through, then headed back to the shoot. He and his crew worked the rest of the afternoon and only stopped when the daylight began to fade. It took another hour to pack up all their gear and head back to the hotel.

"Who wants to go to dinner before heading back to Houston?" Brigitte asked.

Paul, the videographer from the Fairchild shoot, said he'd go if she was agreeable to Mexican.

"How about you, John?"

"I don't know. I might just go home."

When he entered the hotel lobby, he stopped short. Phil was sitting on one of the couches, obviously waiting for him. "Phil! What are *you* doing here? Has something happened?" Visions of Jen in an accident, his father having a heart attack or some other catastrophe raced through his mind.

"Nothing bad has happened," Phil said, rising to meet him. "Can we go up to your room? I have something to show you, and I'd rather do it in private."

"Sure."

They rode the elevator up to the sixth floor, where John's room was located. John was extremely curious but not worried. He figured whatever it was Phil wanted to show him, it was personal.

Inside John's room, he waved Phil to the only chair and he sat on the bed. "So what's so important it couldn't wait until I got back?"

In answer, Phil held out a folded sheet of paper.

John frowned a little and opened it. It took him a few seconds to realize it was an e-mail from Claudia to him. An e-mail that Phil had opened! As he began to read, his heart started to pound. At first, he couldn't concentrate on what she was saying because he was so conscious of Phil sitting there and the fact that Phil had read this, too.

But then her words began to sink in. When he read the end, something inside him expanded. *I wanted you to make love to me. I've wanted that for a long time.* He swallowed.

Slowly, he lowered the paper. His eyes met Phil's. John wasn't sure what he had expected to see there— anger, censure, disappointment, resentment, or maybe even something stronger. But he saw none of those emotions. Instead, Phil gave him a resigned smile.

"She's right, you know. She never *did* belong to me," he said.

John didn't know what to say.

"How long have you been in love with her?"

He deserves an honest answer. "Since the first day I set eyes on her."

Phil nodded.

"I'm sorry, Phil. I never meant to hurt you."

"I know that."

"I fought against what I was feeling. I—I never would have acted on those feelings, either, except you asked me to go see her. That's what opened the floodgates. I mean, I never so much as kissed her before that day, and I never told her how I felt."

"So what are you going to do?" Phil said.

"Do?"

"Yeah, do. You love her, and it's obvious she loves you, so what are you going to do?"

"I—I don't know. I haven't had time to…I mean, how do *you* feel—"

"Believe me," Phil said, interrupting, "if the shoe were on the other foot, if she loved me and not you, I sure as hell wouldn't hesitate to stake my claim. Even if I knew you wanted her, too."

At first John was afraid to believe Phil meant what he was saying.

Then Phil said, "What are you *waiting* for?"

Fifteen minutes later, John had packed and checked out.

Five minutes after that, he was on his way.

Claudia was thinking of putting some bubble bath in the tub and having a long, relaxing soak. She was tired from shopping and cleaning and thinking about the e-mail she'd sent and what John's reaction would be when he read it.

Maybe he's read it already.

But if that were the case, why hadn't she heard from him? Worrying about the e-mail and wondering if she'd done the right thing in sending it had drained Claudia emotionally.

And now it was raining, which didn't help.

When the doorbell rang at eight-thirty, she groaned. Who could *that* be? If it was a salesman, she wouldn't open the door. Glad the hallway was dark, she tiptoed to the door and peered out the peephole.

Her heart slammed in her chest. It was John!

Her hands were shaking as she undid the lock and opened the door.

"I got your e-mail," he said. Drops of water were beaded on his black leather jacket and in his hair.

She just stood there, staring at him.

"Can I come in?"

She nodded and stood back. She still hadn't said a word and she wasn't sure she could. Her insides were one huge trembling mass of protoplasm.

Inside, he took off his jacket and hung it on the clothes tree in the corner. Then he turned to her. "Let's go sit in the living room, okay?"

She swallowed. "Okay."

Once they were seated—this time on the couch—he began to talk. When he got to the part about Phil seeing her e-mail, she cringed. But then he went on, and slowly, her heart filled with hope.

"And then Phil asked me what I was waiting for."

Claudia couldn't have spoken if her life depended on it.

John took her hand. "Claudia, I love you. I think I've loved you from the first day I met you. And if you'll marry me, I promise to love you and be faithful to you until the day I die."

Claudia's heart rocketed with joy. She threw herself into John's arms, nearly knocking him over in the process, and kissed him and kissed him and kissed him.

"I take it that's a yes," he said, laughing as she finally let him up for air.

Later, after they'd gone upstairs and had that bubble bath together, they ordered a gigantic cheese-and-mushroom pizza and talked for hours.

"I want a small wedding," Claudia said.

"I knew you were a girl after my own heart," John said. He plumped up his pillow and drew her into his arms.

"But we'll probably get an argument from my family."

John shrugged. "It's our wedding."

"I know, but you don't know my mother."

He grinned. "Which reminds me, when will I get to meet them?"

"How about this coming weekend? You can go home with me and we'll tell them together."

"Okay."

"And what about *your* family? When are we going to tell them?" She snuggled deeper into his arms.

"How about tomorrow afternoon? I'll tell my mom I'm bringing you for dinner. We'll tell them there." He grinned. "My mother's going to do the happy dance.

I think she thought I'd never get married." He smiled slyly. "She is dying for grandchildren. That's what we need to talk about."

"Why? Don't *you* want children?" Claudia asked.

"I'd love to have a dozen, but kidney disease can cause problems. What if I can't give you any?"

Claudie didn't hesitate. "Then we'll adopt."

John slowly smiled. "You're wonderful, you know that, don't you?"

"I'm not wonderful," Claudia protested.

"Not only wonderful—perfect!"

Claudia was so happy she couldn't stand it. "Have I told you lately that I love you?" she said, running her fingers through his springy chest hair. She loved chest hair. Actually, she loved everything about John, including his crooked toes, which she'd only discovered tonight.

"If you tell me again, I'll make love to you again." He slipped his hand under the covers and stroked her breast.

Claudia closed her eyes, and as their lips met, she decided she was the luckiest girl in the world.

Three weeks later

"But Mother, I don't *want* a big, splashy wedding. John and I talked it over, and we both agree. We want a small wedding with just family and a few close friends."

"That's ridiculous, Claudia," her mother said. "Your grandmother and I have talked, too, and we're of the same mind. Certain things are expected of a young woman in your position."

"I don't care. My wedding is *mine,* and I do not want a society circus."

"It will not be, as you call it, a *circus,*" her mother said in that infuriating tone of voice that said she knew best and would not tolerate any opposition. "It will be beautiful and tasteful and something you'll remember the rest of your life."

"I'll remember a small, intimate wedding even more. And it's what we *want.*"

"There are more people to consider here than just you. Now stop arguing with me, because you are not going to win this one. You will have the kind of wedding that is expected of a Hathaway, and there will be no more discussion."

Claudia stared at her mother. *There will be no more discussion?* Just what did her mother think? That Claudia was just going to roll over and play dead? Well, of course, that's exactly what she thought, because when Kathleen Hathaway set her mind to something, most people did just roll over and die. *Well, she's met her match in me,* Claudia thought. *I don't want a circus—and no matter what she chooses to call it, if I do it her way, it* will *be a circus.*

"I've already called and booked the country club for October tenth." Kathleen walked over and fiddled with the arrangement of flowers that always sat on top of the piano. Her stance said *I'm finished*.

"That's ridiculous! John and I absolutely don't want to wait till October," Claudia said. "We know we need to wait…because of Dad, but want to be married no later than April."

"That is ridiculous, Claudia. April is less than five months away. I can't imagine what you're thinking."

"That's because you're not listening." Claudia was exasperated. In fact, she wanted to scream. Where was John when she needed him?

"Will someone please tell me what all the commotion is about?"

Claudia turned to see her grandmother, with the aid of a cane—her only concession to her age—walking slowly into the drawing room. "Sorry, Gran. Mother and I just can't seem to agree when it comes to my wedding."

Her grandmother's gaze, still bright, fastened itself on Claudia's face. "On what don't you agree?"

"On everything," Claudia said.

"Claudia doesn't want a big wedding," Kathleen said. "And she has some ridiculous notion she can be married in April."

"Nonsense," Claudia's grandmother said. "A proper wedding takes at least six to eight months to plan. Why, it'll take months to get your gown designed and ordered."

"Designed!" Claudia said. "I don't need a designer gown. I can find any number of suitable dresses off the rack in any bridal shop."

"As if any daughter of mine is going to wear an off-the-rack wedding dress," Kathleen scoffed.

Claudia couldn't listen to any more. If she did, she was afraid she would say something she would be sorry for. "Look, we're getting nowhere, and I'm supposed to meet John in Austin in less than an hour and a half. We'll both be back tomorrow, and then we can settle this." Claudia supposed it was cowardly to want John's support, but being a lone voice against both her mother and grandmother, she felt not just outnumbered, but outclassed.

She hurried up to her suite of rooms, grabbed her overnight bag—which she'd packed earlier—her purse and a jacket, then escaped through the back door so she wouldn't have to contend with anything else from either her mother or her grandmother.

It took almost the entire hour and a half to get to the restaurant where she and John were having dinner with Sally. Traffic was always miserable at Christmastime, and now, with only a couple of days left to shop, it seemed as if every single person who lived in Austin was on the roads.

But finally she reached the restaurant. Sally and John were already there, and both stood and hugged and kissed her.

"Oh, you look wonderful," Sally said. "Love agrees with you."

"Yes, it does," Claudia said, smiling at John.

The three of them talked and ordered and talked some more. Once their food arrived, Sally introduced the subject of the wedding. "I'm thrilled that I'm going to be your maid of honor."

"I wouldn't have anyone else," Claudia said.

"Is your cousin going to be your best man?" Sally asked John. Her voice was casual but Claudia knew she was acutely interested in the answer.

"I couldn't have anyone else, either," John said.

"And he's okay with you two getting together," Sally said, more statement than question.

"Seems to be just fine," John said. "He's already dating someone else."

"Oh, no!" Sally said, then blushed. "I was hoping maybe…" Her voice trailed off. She sighed. "Who's he dating?"

"His assistant at the school," Claudia said. She couldn't believe how well things seemed to be working out. Then she frowned, remembering the argument with her mother.

"What's wrong?" John said.

Claudia couldn't help smiling. Sometimes it amazed her that he was so in tune to every nuance of her expression or tone of voice and instantly knew when something was wrong. She related what had happened earlier.

"You know," he said, "even though I don't want a big wedding, if that'll make your family happy, I can live with it."

Claudia reached over and kissed his cheek. "You are the sweetest man in the world."

Sally made a face. "Would you quit smooching? You're making me jealous."

Later, after they'd said goodbye to Sally and were headed to their hotel—they'd decided to spend the night in Austin so they could finish up their Christmas shopping the following day—Claudia brought up the subject of the wedding again.

"I really don't want to give in to my mother," she said. "I want our wedding to be *ours.* And I don't want hundreds of expensive gifts we don't need. I'd rather take the thirty or forty thousand dollars it'll cost and donate it to the Goodfellows where it'll do some real good."

John didn't answer for a while. When he did, his voice was thoughtful. "Claudia, you know I don't care much about your money, don't you?"

"Yes." And she *did* know. He had fallen in love with her before he had any clue who she was.

"But I'm not averse to spending it if it makes you happy."

Now she frowned. "What do you mean?"

"I have an idea."

"Okay."

"Why don't we call the airlines, find out who has a flight to Hawaii in the morning, buy two first-class tickets, and elope?"

"Oh, John," she breathed. "Do…do you mean it?"

"Yeah, I do."

Claudia swallowed. Could she do it? Could she withstand her mother's wrath? And wouldn't Lorna and Chloe and Bryce and Amy and the girls be terribly disappointed? "What about Jen and your family? Won't they be terribly disappointed?"

"They'll get over it. Especially when I explain why we did it. Plus, Mom can have a party for us when we get back. And your mother can do the same thing. If she wants to have some huge reception after the fact, that's fine."

Claudia slowly grinned. It *would* be fine. She could do a reception after they were married. It was the actual ceremony she wanted to be special. And now, because of John, it would be.

"Have I told you lately that I love you?" she whispered, twining her arms around John's neck.

"Tell me again."

* * * * *

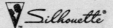

SPECIAL EDITION™

Don't miss a brand-new miniseries
coming to Silhouette Special Edition

THE FORTUNES OF TEXAS: Reunion

HER GOOD FORTUNE

by Marie Ferrarella

Available February 2005
Silhouette Special Edition #1665

Gloria Mendoza had returned to Texas for a
fresh start, and was determined not to get involved
with men. But when bank heir Jack Fortune was
assigned to help with her business affairs and
passion ignited between them, she realized some
vows were meant to be broken....

Fortunes of Texas: Reunion—
The power of family.

Available at your favorite retail outlet.

Silhouette®
Where love comes alive™

If you enjoyed what you just read,
then we've got an offer you can't resist!

Take 2 bestselling
love stories FREE!
Plus get a FREE surprise gift!

Clip this page and mail it to Silhouette Reader Service™

IN U.S.A.	IN CANADA
3010 Walden Ave.	P.O. Box 609
P.O. Box 1867	Fort Erie, Ontario
Buffalo, N.Y. 14240-1867	L2A 5X3

YES! Please send me 2 free Silhouette Special Edition® novels and my free surprise gift. After receiving them, if I don't wish to receive anymore, I can return the shipping statement marked cancel. If I don't cancel, I will receive 6 brand-new novels every month, before they're available in stores! In the U.S.A., bill me at the bargain price of $4.24 plus 25¢ shipping and handling per book and applicable sales tax, if any*. In Canada, bill me at the bargain price of $4.99 plus 25¢ shipping and handling per book and applicable taxes**. That's the complete price and a savings of at least 10% off the cover prices—what a great deal! I understand that accepting the 2 free books and gift places me under no obligation ever to buy any books. I can always return a shipment and cancel at any time. Even if I never buy another book from Silhouette, the 2 free books and gift are mine to keep forever.

235 SDN DZ9D
335 SDN DZ9E

Name	(PLEASE PRINT)	
Address	Apt.#	
City	State/Prov.	Zip/Postal Code

Not valid to current Silhouette Special Edition® subscribers.

Want to try two free books from another series?
Call 1-800-873-8635 or visit www.morefreebooks.com.

* Terms and prices subject to change without notice. Sales tax applicable in N.Y.
** Canadian residents will be charged applicable provincial taxes and GST.
All orders subject to approval. Offer limited to one per household.
® are registered trademarks owned and used by the trademark owner and or its licensee.

SPED04R   ©2004 Harlequin Enterprises Limited

eHARLEQUIN.com

The Ultimate Destination for Women's Fiction

Visit eHarlequin.com's Bookstore today for today's most popular books at great prices.

- An extensive selection of romance books by top authors!

- Choose our convenient "bill me" option. No credit card required.

- New releases, Themed Collections and hard-to-find backlist.

- A sneak peek at upcoming books.

- Check out book excerpts, book summaries and Reader Recommendations from other members and post your own too.

- Find out what everybody's reading in Bestsellers.

- Save BIG with everyday discounts and exclusive online offers!

- Our Category Legend will help you select reading that's exactly right for you!

- Visit our Bargain Outlet often for huge savings and special offers!

- Sweepstakes offers. Enter for your chance to win special prizes, autographed books and more.

Your purchases are 100% guaranteed—so shop online at www.eHarlequin.com today!

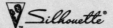

SPECIAL EDITION™

Discover why readers love
Judy Duarte!

From bad boys to heroes...
through the love of a good woman.

The tow-headed son of stunning socialite Kristin Reynolds had to be his. Because, once upon a time, fireman Joe Davenport and Kristin had been lovers, but were pulled apart by her family. Now, they were both adults. Surely Joe could handle parenthood without reigniting his old flame for the woman who tempted him to want the family—and the wife—he could never have.

THEIR SECRET SON
by Judy Duarte
Silhouette Special Edition #1667
On sale February 2005

Meet more Bayside Bachelors later this year!

WORTH FIGHTING FOR—Available May 2005
THE MATCHMAKER'S DADDY—Available June 2005

Only from Silhouette Books!

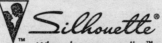

Where love comes alive™

SILHOUETTE *Romance* ®

In a
Fairy Tale
World

Six reluctant couples.

Five classic love stories.

One matchmaking princess.

And time is running out!

Architect Rick Barnett's scars have made him a hard, cynical man. But the innocence of Cynthia Forsythe calls to him. The shadows of the night may disguise the desire in his eyes, but he's still the brooding bad boy who once stole Cynthia's heart…and she's still the good girl whose love could bring him out of the darkness.

NIGHTTIME SWEETHEARTS
by Cara Colter

Silhouette Romance #1754

On sale February 2005!

Only from Silhouette Books!

The world's bestselling romance series.

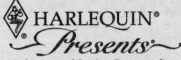

HARLEQUIN®
Presents

Seduction and Passion Guaranteed!

FROM BOARDROOM TO BEDROOM

**Harlequin Presents® brings you two
original stories guaranteed to make
your Valentine's Day extra special!**

THE BOSS'S MARRIAGE ARRANGEMENT
by *Penny Jordan*

Pretending to be her boss's mistress is one thing—but now
everyone in the office thinks Harriet is Matthew Cole's
fiancée! Harriet has to keep reminding herself it's all just
for convenience, but how far is Matthew prepared to go
with the arrangement—marriage?

HIS DARLING VALENTINE
by *Carole Mortimer*

It's Valentine's Day, but Tazzy Darling doesn't care.
Until a secret admirer starts bombarding her with gifts!
Any woman would be delighted—but not Tazzy. There's
only one man she wants to be sending her love tokens, and
that's her boss, Ross Valentine. And her secret admirer
couldn't possibly be Ross…could it?

The way to a man's heart…is through the bedroom